BECAUSE MY DESTINY AWAITS

Corwin McGinnis

MADE FOR SUCCESS

Made for Success Publishing
P.O. Box 1775 Issaquah, WA 98027
www.MadeForSuccess.com

Distributed by Blackstone Publishing

First Printing

Library of Congress Cataloging-in-Publication data

McGinnis, Corwin
    Because My Destiny Awaits
        p. cm.

LCCN: 2024934362
ISBN: 978-1-64146-844-2 *(PBBK)*
ISBN: 978-1-64146-845-9 *(eBook)*
ISBN: 978-1-64146-854-1 *(AUDIO)*

Printed in the United States of America

For further information contact Made for Success Publishing
+1425-526-6480 or email service@madeforsuccess.net

Dedicated to my daughter Destiny.
As you know this book was written for you.
I hope you enjoy it.

Love Dad

CHAPTER ONE

June 20th, 1952

The moment the young girl stepped into the morning, she knew. She just knew. It was going to be a day that would be properly embraced by the young, occasionally remembered by the old, and simply passed through by almost everyone else. It was a Friday, but not just any Friday. It also happened to be the last day of school for the year. The day to follow was June 21st, the first day of summer.

When she left her home that morning, she took a deep breath, paused to consider, then glanced at the sky. Perfect.

The sky was almost entirely clear, revealing the most unique shade of blue, with just enough clouds to make things interesting. She spun a circle in her front yard fast enough to raise the bottom of her new yellow dress almost to her knees. Her mom had ordered the dress from the Sears and Roebuck catalog some two months earlier, and it had arrived the day before. Without much effort, she was granted permission from her mother to wear her white sandals, intended only for church on Sundays, along with her new dress—a first.

While walking on the sidewalk toward her school that morning, although fully unintentional on her part, she couldn't help but notice that each step she took was perfectly timed to miss every crack. Something that her mother's back would much appreciate later that evening.

The wind at her back not only kept her cool and comfortable, but it also finished drying her hair from her morning bath, yet was kind enough to leave most of the smell from her strawberry shampoo. She looked, felt, and even smelled great.

She took a few steps, then a couple more. Suddenly, a cloud moved, and the sun became brighter and warmer, causing a golden mirage to appear on the sidewalk ahead. However, this mirage was of a magical variety in more ways than one. It did not move and was quite possibly attainable.

She kept going. It was still there. Less than a minute later, she stooped to pick up her prize penny, and of course, it was facing heads side up. After further observation, she noticed its mint date to be 1941. The year of her birth. For today, it just had to be.

Moments later, she walked through the school's front doors, which happened to be propped open. Another first. More than likely, the doors had been left in this position as a greeting for the young girl, though most thought they welcomed the warm, flower-scented summer air.

As soon as she entered her classroom, her teacher, a smiling Ms. McCormick, asked, "Ruby, is that a new dress?" The bell that had been patiently waiting rang, drowning out the obvious answer and keeping her modesty afloat. She found her report card when she reached her desk, straight A's. Joy bloomed inside her as she looked to the ceiling and smiled.

It was the early 1950s and probably one of our country's most preferred times to come of age if the choice could be made. The calendars of the depression, which had kept the fires lit during the Second World War, had long since turned to ash and had been discarded, although not forgotten, into flowerbeds near the hearth. They would provide nutrition for the flowers that, in turn, would provide much-needed hope to a waiting, soon-to-be remarkable generation.

I Love Lucy was the top show on television, followed by *Dragnet*. Rocky Marciano was currently the top heavyweight boxing champion and would eventually retire undefeated. Elvis Presley, soon to be known as "The King of Rock and Roll," was young, standing in line, waiting his turn to take the stage. His crown was starting to be forged and would be waiting for him in Memphis.

These moments were not taken for granted by the young girl. She knew they were more than black and white pictures in the family photo album, which would be glanced at briefly on rainy days before turning the page, hoping for the showers to refrain so life could once again resume.

The girl, Ruby, could be found outdoors in such weather. Looking up, never down, and feeling the drops on her face, which could be mistaken for tears if you didn't know the weather, or the girl.

Later in the afternoon, on that last day of school for the year, Ruby rode her bike to her favorite place in her small world called Lost Lake. The lake was almost perfectly egg-shaped except for the very bottom, where it appeared someone had taken a bite out of it when it was being formed. Steep hills surrounded and protected the peaceful waters, creating a small valley deterring those lacking ambition and helping to maintain its secrecy.

Ruby obviously didn't mind this feature as it gave her much-needed and appreciated privacy. A little more than a hundred years earlier, a family of settlers who also recognized the hill's value didn't mind the difficult climb either. A small, deteriorating log cabin twenty yards from the shore was proof. Over time, one of the logs from the cabin had broken free and rolled toward the water's edge, perhaps out of thirst or in hopes of a swim. Luckily for Ruby, it didn't reach its goal, and the log became her favorite resting place near the lake.

Ruby enjoyed sitting on the log and taking in the area's wildlife, both animals and plants. The early settlers had been thoughtful enough to plant apple trees, which grew sporadically throughout the valley. Although they hadn't been pruned in decades, they still produced many delicious varieties when they had a mind to. For some reason, rainbows were nearly a daily occurrence at Lost Lake, which seemed almost mystical because the rains were few and far between.

Each day, when Ruby first arrived at the water's edge, she'd sit on her log and then close her eyes. Next, she'd take and release the deepest of breaths that she could. Early on, she had become aware that all nature is connected, or perhaps the awareness was more of a memory.

Her inward breaths contained gratitude and requests. Her outgoing breaths were filled with help and unconditional love for all who had a need and a desire to accept it.

With her eyes still closed, Ruby was able to see the wind, not needing proof from the rustling of leaves, the swaying grass, or its feel upon her face. She could just see. Also, with her eyes still closed, she could sense the presence of the small dancing lights that surrounded her. She could feel their warmth, protection, and guidance. She didn't know if these were the candles of the early settlers, nor did it matter. She knew that the wind, her wind, had no desire to blow them out. They were and always would be.

Of all the animals that lived in the area, Ruby was most attracted to the birds. Her favorite was a bald eagle. Nearly every evening, the majestic bird could be counted upon to make an appearance. He knew that as the leader of the small valley, it was his responsibility to oversee and make sure that all was well. Blessed with vision five times that of man, this was a fairly easy task for the distinguished bird. High above the land, humbly relying on the sweet, gentle breaths of angels and the occasional flapping of his wings, the eagle soared and observed. After validating that the scale of justice for all who lived below was once again nearly whole and true, he took command of gravity. Combining his great strength and vision, he made a vertical beeline below the water's surface. A split second later, the eagle crossed the water's surface, this time in the opposite direction, proudly displaying the sacrifice for the evening, a German brown trout in his beak. Moments later, this vacancy was filled when the next infant resident of Lost Lake appeared and took its turn. Satisfied that balance had been restored, the bald eagle flew off, looking forward to the night's meal and much-appreciated rest.

The youngster who arrived that evening was a white baby snow goose. The technical name is "gosling," but baby goose sounds so much better. Don't you think?

For some reason, the little fellow, dressed only in a thin layer of down, was all alone. It was quite possible that he had lost his way. Whatever the reason for his being alone, quite understandably, fear and darkness crept over the baby goose simultaneously that night.

After experiencing the cold and the frightening noises of the night for the first time, the little goose was beside himself when the sun finally began to show, accompanied by the welcoming and friendly chirping of the early morning birds. Instinctively, he made his way toward the lake in need of a drink.

Upon his arrival, fate let its wisdom be known. Lo and behold, there was a mother goose along with six babies milling around the water's edge. This was a family of Canadian Geese whose down was a combination of dark green and yellow.

Assuming his own and out of a desperate need to belong, he went straight toward the others. Recognizing that the late arrival was albino and that seven is definitely an odd number, the others took to shooing him away. Accepting that the cold shoulders, or wings, I should say, were more welcome than a scary, frigid night all alone in the woods, the little snow goose accepted his position and stayed as close as he could to the others yet still far enough away to be considered an outcast.

That night, although he was the furthest away from Mother Goose in the nest, he appreciated what warmth he received and was thankful for having found a place to belong.

The next day, Ruby was pleased as fruit punch when she saw the white baby goose coming out of the woods along with his adoptive family. Of course, she noticed his treatment by the others, and her heart went out to him. She immediately said a prayer out of the utmost selflessness. Here was her request: "Dear Lord, this may sound crazy, but I ask you to make the little snow goose colorblind. Please, Lord . . ."

The superior logic of the child was that each time he went to drink from the lake, his reflection wouldn't reveal his difference from the others. As we all know, it was too late for this, but her innocence and selflessness were priceless, were they not?

The arrival of the mixed family of geese to Lost Lake during her visits became the highlight of Ruby's days. She'd always root for the underdog, of course. It bothered her to see the snow goose being pushed to the outskirts and having to eat from the thinnest patches of grass. He was always the last to get his drink from the lake and the last in line when the family walked home.

That fall, when it was time for the geese to head for warmer weather, this was the family's flight formation: Mother Goose was at the helm with three biological goslings to her left and three biological goslings to her right. Then there was the step-gosling, who was positioned at the far right and to the rear, causing the whole thing to look wonky and out of balance.

However, things began to change that winter for the baby snow goose. Gradually, the shooing away and unwelcomeness within the clique of the "cool kids" began to have an interesting effect on the young bird. He slowly became more resilient, and he began to grow.

On the way home to Lost Lake the next spring, our little hero in white moved up two spots in the formation, although he took the promotion in all modesty.

When Ruby saw him for the first time that year, she couldn't believe her eyes. His neck was much thicker than the others, and he was a full head taller. Of course, she bowed her head, whispering, "Thank you, Lord . . ."

She then excitedly looked up to observe. At just a year old, the young geese had all gradually learned the meaning of respect. Now, when it was time to eat, the biological goslings purposely left the tallest and lushest grass for the step-gosling. He took a drink from the lake whenever he wanted, never having to wait.

A lot of individuals would have reacted differently to the change in the family's dynamics. Perhaps others would remember the outcast status and return similar treatment, but this was not the case. The snow goose slowly and humbly accepted his leadership position.

His poor treatment was not forgotten, of course, and it actually became a reminder to help those in similar situations, including those outside his family.

That fall, the snow goose, who had formed a bond with Ruby, having instinctively felt her concern, purposely waited for her appearance when it was time for him to fly south again.

Our hero and his brothers and sisters floated on the surface of Lost Lake that morning. His siblings were eager to get started on their long journey, and they let it be known, but only softly, mind you. The snow goose sternly but kindly explained the importance of his bidding farewell to Ruby. Upon her arrival, he engaged the others in small talk, allowing the young girl to complete her ritual of closed-eye breathing exercises. Then, it was time.

The large bird swam to the shore and approached Ruby, coming within a yard of the girl who, earlier in the summer, had celebrated her twelfth birthday. He then bowed his head to his friend. The two of them were able to hear nature's standing ovation: the chirping of the other birds and the sound of the waves happily reaching their destination, signifying our hero's ability to overcome status and accept responsibility for the future.

He winked at Ruby, then turned away and began to fly off. His siblings happily joined him to the rear, evenly distributed three to the left and three to the right. Mother Goose, who was getting along in years, decided not to make the journey south that year.

What a vision, a majestic white goose in the first position with six now-brown Canadian geese flying proudly behind their leader. The sight brought tears to Ruby's eyes. It was one of those moments in someone's life that are impossible to forget. Not wanting to rush the moment, Ruby allowed time and evaporation, not the wiping of her hands, to dry her eyes. Once her sight was restored, she was once again pleased as punch, this time strawberry, by the large white feather that lay on the ground directly in front of her.

As the years went on, Ruby's visits to Lost Lake weren't as frequent as they were in her youth. However, from time to time, when she did make the trip and the two friends did see one another, they greatly enjoyed catching up. There are few higher honors in life than when nature welcomes man, or woman, into her midst. Because of this understanding and their friendship, Ruby never forgot that as you make your way and experience those brief, rare moments in your life when you are all alone outdoors, and it suddenly becomes unusually quiet, and you see a white feather gently dancing down the invisible stairwell from above, that someone in white who has quite possibly overcome more difficulties than you, is always thinking about and watching over you.

She never took these moments for granted.

CHAPTER TWO

Present Day, Washington State

Night had fallen over the city of Tacoma. A blanket of black hung from above, worn slightly in spots. Behind one of these areas, between the threads of darkness, light emerged from a young girl's bedroom.

Eleven-year-old Jojo Cobbler was resting in her bed, rapidly becoming tired and awaiting the entrance of her mother, Brenda. Not a night goes by without the mother and daughter joining together to say prayers. Jojo yawned a couple of times, then slipped away, falling asleep. A dream began in her mind, but before it became clear, or any part could be remembered, Brenda entered and said, "Wake up, sweetheart, time for prayers."

Jojo woke up from a slight fog, smiled at her mother, and they began.

"Now I lay me down to sleep . . ." The pair continued, and at the end, they both paused. Silently, each one made their own wishes and thanks to God.

"Amen."

"Amen."

"I love you, Mom, g'night," Jojo said.

"Love you too, kiddo. Good night," Brenda replied.

"Could you please open the window a little bit? I'm too warm," Jojo added.

"Again tonight? It doesn't feel that warm to me, but okay," Brenda answered. Jojo pulled the blankets up to her nose. She didn't want her mom to know she was smiling. It really wasn't too warm. She just enjoyed the sounds of the outdoors. At night, she would listen patiently until she heard the "Who, who, whooo" of an old owl that visited her regularly from a tree in her yard.

"Who, who, who" is the only word owls seem to know. The old owl would let Jojo know he was there by his only lonely word.

The owl would eventually fly off. The sound of his wings was the last thing that Jojo would hear as she fell asleep. The owl's departure meant another day was being put to memory.

Most mornings, the young girl was awakened by the owl's friends, the morning birds, and today was no different. A smile came to her face before her heavy eyes opened. Rubbing her eyes awake, Jojo quickly left her bed for the sights and sounds that her window offered. The birds' morning greetings brought happiness and hope to the start of each new day. Jojo could barely make out their shapes as they bounced from limb to limb on their favorite tree. Darkness slowly gave way to the power of the sun.

Now, Jojo was resourceful as well as very kind. She knew mornings meant breakfast, and she wished to help the birds find their morning meal. Remembering that her father, Trevor, had tilled a couple of flower-beds the previous day, she went outside in search of the bird's favorite food.

Still in her pajamas, forgetting socks and shoes, Jojo's feet became damp and cold as she stepped onto the yard's moist grass. However, her cold feet were quickly forgotten when she began looking under dirt clods and rocks in the flowerbeds for worms.

The unexpecting dirt crawlers gave up quickly; however, a few were pinched in half while trying to make their escape as Jojo gathered them for her friends, the morning birds. With six different-sized worms in one hand and eight and a half in the other, she marched to the family's picnic table and spread out her slimy gifts.

Jojo went back inside to the window in her room to watch the birds fly down and hungrily swallow their first meal of the day. She was glad to have helped and enjoyed watching her winged friends fly down, land, and then leave. Occasionally, their beaks happily displayed the ends of the squirming worms. Some were en route to their nests to feed their young.

What she didn't realize was that her bare feet left a dirty trail to her bedroom door, which became lighter and lighter with every step. Jojo's mother noticed these dirty prints on a regular basis, but she never mentioned them to her daughter. Truly, there are few secrets in families.

Jojo then laid back down on her bed, her head resting on a pillow, staring up at the ceiling but not really seeing. Just looking. Lost in thought, she began drifting . . . and drifting . . . Once again, she was digging worms; this time, however, she was being helped by an older man who might have been related to her, but that of an age that made him seem almost Biblical. After finishing this task, and a pact of sorts having been sealed, Jojo found herself walking through a celebration and holding hands with another elder, again quite possibly a family member; this time, however, they were female.

While some memories can be misplaced for a time, they are never truly forgotten, and you never know when they may work themselves free. In a flash, they can once again surface, coming from the strangest of places. For example, from within our dreams, the dreams of others, or even the dreams of our children.

"Jojo, Jojo . . . It's time to wake up, sweetheart." Young Jojo was awakened by her mother, who brought in her little brother, one-year-old Hudson, to crawl around on her bed. Her brother was rather hyper at this time of day. He was well-rested, hungry, and thankful to be rid of the boundaries of his crib that contained him throughout the night.

Jojo was a little groggy at first, then began displaying her uncontrollable smile. She had an awareness inside that not nearly enough of us have. Life is a precious gift. Each moment itself is a treasure. The map to this treasure lies inside all our hearts. We just need to look.

Brenda began slowly explaining the day's upcoming events, which she and Trevor had planned the night before, "After breakfast, you're going to turn in your homeschool assignment, then the three of us are going to The Garden Store to pick up some bulbs, seeds, and other things for the flowerbeds that Dad got ready yesterday. I thought it would be nice to work in the yard this afternoon. I know how much you and your brother enjoy the outdoors."

Jojo's contagious smile spread to Hudson, causing him to crawl straight toward her. Happily, she held him close. She loved going to The Garden Store and could hardly wait. Today was going to be a great day, a happy day, or so she thought.

For breakfast, the family ate pancakes topped with blueberries and finished with a glass of orange juice. Next, Mother gave Hudson a bath and then took one herself. After Jojo finished taking hers and getting dressed, she brushed her teeth and looked at herself in the mirror, making funny faces with her foamy toothpaste mouth. When she was done and had wiped her mouth clean, she continued looking. Her skin was on the pale side, yet she never got sunburned. In fact, she tanned quicker than most. Her eyes were a unique blend of robin's egg blue with highlights of turquoise that appeared stirred in, especially in sunlight. Her hair was naturally blonde and styled in a long bob with a swirl of bubble gum pink and cotton candy blue just peeking out at the ends. She had a thin nose that turned up just a tad at the tip. A funny thing happened to her when it was extremely hot out; her nose actually sweated. Little salty beads could be counted on the surface on days of eighty degrees or greater, just like the rest of her family.

As she continued to look, she wondered, *Am I pretty?*

Her parents said she was, but they had to. Didn't they? She'd never heard of a mother or father telling their kid that they were ugly. But still . . . What about other people? Or, more importantly, *the kids in the neighborhood, at church, or her friends*—What did they think? Deciding that it would be too weird to ask them, she took one last, long look at herself and decided that she wouldn't worry about what other people thought. She then spoke softly so just mirror Jojo could hear, "But, just between you and me, we look good. Dang good!"

She placed her pointer finger up to her lips to signify their secret. She smiled and was out the door.

Jojo went to her bedroom to get the homework assignment that her mother had given her the day before. She brought the paper into the kitchen to find her waiting at the table.

Brenda said, "I see you have your writing assignment, sweetheart. Instead of just turning it in, why don't you read it to me? This will give you practice at speaking in front of others at the same time."

"Sure, Mom," Jojo replied, less than enthusiastically.

While confident in many ways, she was also a little on the shy side. She cleared her throat, which she always did when she was nervous. Her eyes looked down at the floor and inspected her fidgeting feet instead of facing her audience of one.

Brenda spoke reassuringly, "It's okay, Jojo. Look at me and relax. It's just the two of us. Imagine that we are just having a conversation, nothing more. You're going to do great!"

"Okay, Mom, and thanks!" Jojo replied.

She thought, *Smell the flower* as she inhaled, and, *Blow out the candle* as she exhaled. "*Smell the flower, blow out the candle.*" Peace came over Jojo as she began. "My story is called *Hairy Mary.* Mary is a fourth grader in Mrs. Nugent's class at Hunt Elementary School. Mary is nice, smart, and pretty. She has a nickname. The kids in her class call her Hairy Mary. When Mary hands in an assignment, a lot of times, there is a hair or two on the paper. When Mary puts her coat on the back of her chair, there are hairs on it. Bill sits behind Mary. He whispers to Mary and teases her, and says she is going bald. Mary smiles at Bill. She knows she isn't losing her hair. Once when Lisa left her math book at home, Mary shared hers with Lisa. In between the pages they were working on, there were hairs. Lisa told some of the class she thought Mary slept in a barn. Mary smiled at Lisa. She knows she doesn't sleep in a barn.

"Once, Mrs. Nugent had Mary come up in front of the class. There were math problems on the chalkboard. Mrs. Nugent asked Mary to write in the answers. Mary did. She got the answers right, then she went back to her desk. Mrs. Nugent wrote new math problems on the chalkboard. She noticed where Mary had been standing there were a couple of hairs on the floor. Mrs. Nugent didn't say anything but thought to herself, *Poor Mary, she really is hairy.*

"Friday is show and tell. This week, Bill brought his new video game. The boys liked Bill's game. The girls rolled their eyes up like they were looking at their bangs. Next, Lisa showed the class her new jeans. A couple of the girls said they were cute. One girl asked how much they cost. The boys rolled their eyes. Boys don't like girls' jeans. There was a knock on the classroom door. It was Mary's mom. She carried in a big noisy box. It was Mary's turn for show and tell. Mary reached into the box and pulled out one of four puppies.

"'My mom raises puppies,' Mary told everyone. The puppy licked Mary's face and barked playfully at the class. Mary smiled at the puppy. The boys AND the girls liked Mary's puppy!

"'Can we hold them?' asked the class.

"'Of course,' Mary said. The class took turns holding Mary's puppies. The puppies were shedding their hair. All of the kids got puppy hair on themselves. One of Mary's puppies peed on Lisa's new jeans. Since Mary got to play with puppies all the time, she got a new nickname. When Mary came to school on Monday, everyone called her Lucky Mary, everyone except Lisa, that is! Lucky Mary smiled."

"Oh my gosh, Jojo. That was absolutely funny. Great job! You even drew a picture! Is that pee on Lisa's pants? You crazy kid, I'm giving you an A-plus!"

After her mother wrote A-plus-plus in large red markings on the paper, she handed it back to Jojo and said, "Get your brother, kiddo, and we will be on our way."

Next, the family went outside and got into their SUV. After buckling up for safety, the trio drove to The Garden Store.

CHAPTER THREE

As soon as they entered the store, Jojo went straight to the exotic birds the store offered. She enjoyed a talking parrot, although he never wanted to repeat any of her suggestions. A variety of other singing, chirping, and tweeting birds seemed to show off for her attention. Her eyes danced from cage to cage, very pleased to see and hear the bouncing feathered critters. The birds mesmerized her.

Brenda knew right where to find her daughter. Pushing Hudson in a shopping cart, she startled Jojo when she spoke up from behind her, "I know you love them, kid, but please remember we aren't buying any birds." Mother knew Jojo all too well. "I'm just checking on you. I need to pick up the things on my list. Do you want to stay here with the birds or come with your brother and me?" Brenda asked.

"I'll stay here, Mom," Jojo answered.

"Okay, sweetie, we'll come back and get you before we check out," Brenda replied.

When she started pushing the cart away, Hudson spoke, "Bir-bir, bir-bir." His hands reached toward the caged birds. Mother and Jojo both knew what Hudson meant.

"Yes, Hudson, those are birds, alright. We have a couple of things to pick up. We'll come back in a few and see them when we pick up sister," their mom explained.

"Yep," Hudson replied. He showed a disappointed look as he rode away in the cart.

Jojo's thoughts returned to the birds. She day-dreamed of all the colorful birds living free in her backyard. She thought of teaching the parrot words and phrases. What a surprise Mother would have if the parrot joined them at the window one night while they said their prayers. This idea and many others came to Jojo. She often used her imagination as another way to look at things.

While Jojo's eyes drifted from cage to cage, she noticed someone approaching from her right.

"How's my favorite youngster today?" asked the now-familiar Mr. Dennis.

"Great! Oh man, hi, Mr. Dennis," Jojo answered. Mr. Dennis owned The Garden Store. He was an extremely nice man, dressed in coveralls and a red and black flannel shirt that reminded Jojo of a checkerboard. He was completely bald except for a small patch of wavy white hair above each ear.

The store's owner was very popular with the children of the area. He carried a pocketful of candy that, with parents' approval, was offered to all kids as they readied to leave his store. During the drive home, the sweet, sticky gifts usually flavored the children's mouths. Sometimes, however, those leaving The Garden Store in the latter part of the day were encouraged by their parents to save their candy until they got home. Mr. Dennis' candy became rather sticky by day's end, having been kept in his pocket all day. No one dared tell the kind man this, although numerous families had souvenirs embedded in their car's carpets, reminding them of the sticky treats. Often, when children came home with tales of candy stuck to their faces, hands, and clothes, few could deny a visit to The Garden Store.

Mr. Dennis also dressed as Santa Claus for Christmas each year. He made sure every child visiting his store during the season received a wrapped gift from one of two cloth bags kept behind the counter. A blue one for the boys and red for the girls. Last year, Jojo received a doll similar to a Barbie.

Brenda returned to her daydreaming daughter, who had not moved from the caged birds since her arrival. Hudson's eyes lit up at the sight of the birds. Giving him a chance to observe, Mother waited a short while before saying, "Time to go, kids."

"K," replied Jojo, her eyes still locked on her friends. Taking the girl by the hand, Mother slowly pried the child out of her trance. Hudson looked over his shoulder and waved goodbye to the birds as they made their way to the cash register. The Cobblers paid for their items. Jojo and Hudson gladly received a piece of candy from the smiling Mr. Dennis. Butterscotch was the award today.

CHAPTER FOUR

After driving a couple of blocks away from The Garden Store, the Cobbler family could hear sirens coming from behind them. Because of this, Brenda obediently pulled the family's SUV to the right side of the road along with the other motorists. Quickly, the sirens became louder and louder as they upheld their responsibility of clearing the way for their maker, a fast-traveling white police car that proceeded past the Cobblers, boasting its flashing red and blue lights along the way. Just as fast as they arrived, the sirens began to quiet as the police raced toward the emergency that commanded their attention.

Soon, another wave of sirens and lights approached as the next police car came into the scene and left just as quickly as the first, then another. The Cobblers continued to listen. A long, quiet pause occurred within the small family's SUV. After the family listened patiently for more than a minute, it became clear that there would not be any more sirens. So, Brenda took charge and initiated the next conversation, "Well, guys, what do you say we start heading the rest of the way home now?" The brother and sister looked at one another.

Jojo replied, "Do you think they were chasing bad guys, Mom?"

"You just never know, kiddo. They could be chasing bad guys, or there could be an accident up ahead, or a medical emergency, or maybe a fire. A lot of times, we never find out what the emergency truly is if it doesn't make the news," she answered.

This time was going to be different. They were definitely going to find out the nature of the emergency. When the Cobblers were just a couple of blocks from home, all three police cars came into view once

more. As before, they were all topped with red and
blue flashing lights, although the sirens were no longer allowed to voice their opinion. The police cars
were situated to block the suspect's vehicle, which
forced Brenda to stop her SUV in the middle of the
street and placed them alongside the center of attention—a brown four-door sedan covered in bumper
stickers, with all four doors and the trunk left in their
open positions.

A black man in his mid-forties was lying on the
ground on his stomach. His hands were handcuffed

behind his back, and he wore a white face mask. His head was on the ground, with his right cheek painfully supporting its weight. A kneeling police officer had one of his knees placed in the center of the man's back. He faced the Cobblers. Brenda lowered her window to better hear what was going on. Now that the sirens were mute, angry comments and questions from the police took their place, filling the air.

"Don't move or else, buddy!"

"The Key Bank on 84ᵗʰ and Pacific was just robbed by a black man wearing a mask!"

"We know it was you!"

"Where's the money?"

"Where's the gun?"

"*Well?*"

Momentarily, the police held their questions, allowing the man on the ground to answer. He chose not to. Jojo locked eyes with the man. A single lonely tear rolled down his cheek, then hid behind his mask, quite possibly out of embarrassment. This triggered an emotional outburst inside Jojo, whose eyes also filled with tears. With their eyes still locked, the black man could feel the young girl's compassion and began to let his tears flow uncontrollably as well. Although the shouting and flashing lights continued, filling the moment with extreme tension, somehow, silence engulfed Jojo and the man. They seemed to enter into a brief conversation just between themselves, as if by magic. They spoke through their eyes and thoughts.

I didn't rob no bank, little girl.

I know you didn't, Mister. I can tell your heart is good. I totally believe you. I just feel so sorry for you. Big time!

Thank you so much. You'll see, sweetheart, this is a big misunderstanding. It will all work out. But . . . Still . . . I shouldn't have to go through this in the first place. It's degrading.

I'm sure it is, Mister. I'm sure it is.

Well, I must ask one favor of you, if I may? Please turn your head and look away so I can properly focus on what lies ahead. I must regain my composure and replace my anger and embarrassment with peace, pride, and dignity. Perhaps one day we'll meet again in more favorable conditions. Peace out, little one.

I'd like that, sir, and of course I will. Peace. Then Jojo glanced to the rear of the man's car and began taking inventory of the many bumper stickers that decorated it: Rainiers, Co-Exist, Pro-choice, Black

Lives Matter. There were also many rainbow stickers in different sizes.

Soon, a policeman approached the car and spoke to Brenda, "Thanks for your patience, Ma'am. We are going to be moving the cruiser up ahead so that you can drive through. It's quite possible that we have the wrong man, but we're not one hundred percent sure yet. There's still a lot that needs to be sorted out here."

"Oh, thank you, officer. I do need to get the kids home. They are awfully young to be witnessing all of this. I will have some explaining to do, that's for sure. Good day," she replied. Moments later, the police car blocking the road moved, and the Cobblers continued on.

Not able to contain herself any longer, Jojo blurted out, "Oh, Mom! The poor black man! Why—"

Brenda cut her off, "Things in the world are very complicated right now, Jojo. You won't fully understand until you get older, but I'll do my best to explain. And Hudson, you were such a big boy just now. I'm so proud of you. You did so well!"

Hearing his name pulled Hudson out of the trance he was in from watching *Paw Patrol* on the car's entertainment system. This caused the boy to sit up a little straighter, and he occasionally nodded his head, pretending to understand what his mom was about to share. However, his attention was short-lived, and his loyalty returned to the pups who were about to embark on another adventure.

His mother continued to speak, "There are a lot of bad things taking place in the world right now: prejudice, wars, school shootings, and so much more. Because of this, the police are on edge. Sometimes, they are quite possibly overreacting, and other times, maybe they aren't doing enough. No matter what they do, people are looking to find fault. We have kids desperate for attention and purpose who arm themselves and carry out school shootings, not fully understanding the consequences of their actions, nor realizing that in a couple of years, no one will remember their names or their reasons for what they did. All that remains are lost lives, broken hearts, and shattered families."

Jojo spoke again, eager to learn more. "Mom, what about the man's bumper stickers? What do they mean?"

The family's SUV pulled into their driveway, and Brenda spoke, "I'll do my best to explain the bumper stickers in a few minutes. We still have a lot to do in the yard this afternoon, and we need to get started. Jojo, could you please help bring Hudson into the house?"

"You got it," answered Jojo.

Hudson could walk on his own but was prone to falling down. He hadn't mastered control of his legs yet. Holding his sister's hand gave him better balance. He felt safe. He grinned proudly and made his way into their home without incident.

CHAPTER FIVE

Once inside the house, Brenda began explaining the bumper stickers.

"Okay, kids, I'll do my best to explain what the man's bumper stickers mean. I took pictures with my phone of what was taking place while we waited for the road to open up. I have some photos of his car. I think I have most of his bumper stickers as well. The first one is the easiest, The Rainiers. That's the name of our professional baseball team here in Tacoma. It just so happens that your father's boss recently gave him some free tickets. Soon, we will be going to a game as a family, and you'll be able to experience the Rainiers firsthand. It will be a lot of fun! The others, Co-Exist, Pro-Choice, Black Lives Matter, and the rainbow stickers, are more complicated to understand but extremely important at the same time.

"I'll start with Pro-Choice. The Pro-Choice movement feels that women must always be the ones who decide if they want to have children or not, and that they should be the ones who make all the medical decisions that go along with it. Besides Pro-Choice, there is also Pro-Life, which looks at things a little differently. They like to help in different ways. For example, adoption. If a woman becomes pregnant but isn't ready to be a mother yet, then Pro-Life organizations can help place her child with families who want to have kids but may not be able to on their own. Nice, huh?"

"Sure is," agreed Jojo.

"The rainbow stickers mean that everyone has the right to love whomever they want. Do those make sense so far?"

Jojo's response was an enthusiastic, "Of course!"

Hudson perfectly timed his nod with his sister's answer, which was cute as all get out.

Brenda then suggested, "Hudson, this has to be boring for a little guy like you. How about if I put on *Ms. Rachel* in the living room for you while I finish up with Jojo? Then, we can all go outside." The boy's grin was answer enough. Moments later, his attention was on the *Ms. Rachel* show, and his mother continued her talk with Jojo.

"So, sweetheart, Black Lives Matter is probably one of the most popular statements and movements of the time right now, and rightly so. Our country, and the entire world for that matter, has become aware of extreme discrimination and racism against black people. It began a little over ten years ago, in 2012, when a white man killed a black teenage boy and then was acquitted. Meaning that he didn't get in trouble and go to prison for taking the young man's life. Since then, there have been a number of black men who have been killed by policemen during attempted arrests. These were men who hadn't even been charged with a crime when they were killed at the hands of the police. The reason I'm explaining this to you without Hudson is because he is much too young to be hearing this. Honestly, you are, too, Jojo. But . . . Sooner or later, you will be learning about this, and I'd rather you hear the truth from me, rather than from someone else. That is why I took pictures of the police arresting the man this morning. In case there were any problems, I felt that pictures taken by an impartial witness could be helpful. For the sake of the black man and the police themselves. Make sense?"

"It sure does, Mom! I have heard about Black Lives Matter a bunch of times, but I didn't know what it meant. I should have asked you. Now, knowing about it makes me feel so sad for the people who have been killed! Oh my gosh, Mom, think about their poor families too!" Jojo concluded.

"I know, sweetheart. It sends a negative ripple effect into many more lives than just those that make the news. Are you feeling okay after what you have just learned, Jojo?" Brenda asked her.

"Yes, Mom," Jojo answered.

Brenda hugged her daughter and then pulled back and looked into her eyes reassuringly, then continued, "Okay, kiddo. The last bumper sticker is Co-Exist. It has a couple of meanings. I'd like you to think of it as all people should be able to live in peace with one another and be able to attend the church of their choice. Freedom to choose their own religion. Like how we go to the church we want. Do you agree?"

Jojo replied, "Yeah, I do. I like our church. I have a lot of friends there. I'm happy we get to go there."

Brenda continued, "In a way, excluding the Rainiers bumper sticker, the rest of the man's bumper stickers could be summarized by the golden rule, which is, 'Love your neighbor as yourself.' If everyone felt this way and treated each other like this, from letting women decide if they want to have children or not, to the Black Lives Matter movement, then the world would be a better place than it is right now. It would be safer. People would be happier. Love your neighbor as yourself—Because all lives matter. Your life matters, Jojo." Mother hugged Jojo, then finished, "I sure love you, kiddo."

"Love you too, Mom," Jojo stated, then asked, "You know what, Mom?"

"What's that, honey?" Mom asked.

"I sure hope everything works out for the black man we saw today. I felt a connection with him. I don't think he robbed the bank," Jojo explained.

"I hope for his sake you're right!" Brenda replied.

Lunch consisted of tuna sandwiches, cut diagonally, a family trait. Bananas and orange juice rounded out the meal. After eating, the kids brought their dirty dishes to Brenda, who promptly washed them. When finished with this task, Brenda wiped her hands on her apron and tucked a few strands of her hair behind her ears that had fallen free, then said, "Why don't you two go out back? I'll be out in a minute. Then we'll get started."

Complaisant and anxious, the brother and sister hastily made their way out the back door into their large fenced backyard.

The Cobbler's backyard had been made with children in mind. Trevor and Brenda fashioned this area to include a sandbox, swing set, and a treehouse. A cedar fence lined with flowerbeds decorated the border of the yard, forming a large horseshoe shape. The center was carpeted with dark green grass and included four trees: an apple, a cherry, and two "climbing" trees, one of which contained the treehouse. The trees were where the owl and the morning birds perched and played during their visits.

Jojo and Hudson were waiting near the picnic table when Brenda came out the backdoor carrying two flats; one contained seeds and bulbs, and the other had young flower starts. Hudson happily jumped up and down, clapping his hands together, and landed on his bottom at the sight of his mother, who walked to the picnic table and set the plants down.

Jojo picked up the flat of flowers and breathed in deeply. She discovered it was too early for the plants to offer noses their gifts, but she still held the young flowers below Hudson's nose. Hudson declared, "Mmmm, purdy."

"You're right, Hudson. Flowers do smell pretty. They'll smell even better when they are in full bloom," Brenda advised. "Well, guys, what do you say we get started?"

Agreeing, the children walked with her to one of two recently tilled flowerbeds. Jojo carried the flat of flowers, careful not to spill any. The flimsy box bounced the plants when she walked. After setting the box down, Jojo held Hudson's hand and waited for Mother's instructions.

Both brother and sister looked at one another and smiled. They knew that in just moments, they would be playing in the dirt, getting totally filthy and receiving praise for working in the flowerbeds, both benefits of youth that grownups sometimes call chores.

Using a spade and hoe left near the flowerbed by Father, the three dug holes. They made rows. They planted. Bulbs were placed in well-thought-out locations by Mother. Flower starts were set just so by Jojo. Hudson spread wildflower seeds all over. The small garden would bloom and blossom at different times throughout the upcoming summer and the years to come. The secrets of seed and bulb would be revealed as beautiful colors and smells.

When the flowerbeds had taken shape and were nearing completion, Brenda brought a green hose to the edge of the soil. She would soon be giving Jojo and Hudson the honor and fun of watering the future flowers. The final step. The seed being sown.

"Why don't you two water the flowerbeds real good? I'm going in to start supper. Dad will be home shortly. You guys did an awesome job," Mother complimented them.

"Oh, and don't get each other wet with the hose," she finished with a mischievous smile that contradicted her statement.

As she was leaving the yard to start dinner, Brenda turned on the water spigot and then went into the house to begin cooking. The water traveling down the hose appeared to give it life, lightly expanding and moving it. A giant green rubber snake.

Jojo held the hose first. A rainbow appeared just after the water did. Hudson pointed to the misty colors in the air. A reminder of God's promise to Noah to never flood the entire earth again, one that hasn't, nor ever will be broken. The dirt became darker in the areas touched by the water. Soon, Jojo shared the hose with Hudson. She pointed at his rainbow. She told her brother the names of the different colors. Hudson silently mouthed each word after hearing it from his sister.

When dinner began cooking, Mother re-entered the backyard. Watching her children, she realized her haste and quietly slipped back inside the house to observe from the closest window. She grinned to herself at the sight of her children spending time together and helping one another. Brenda was a special person and mother. She knew times like these fed her children's spirits. All children need, deserve, and must experience days such as these. Aware of life's checks and balances, Brenda felt responsible for creating these necessary moments. These priceless times are automatically deposited into internal savings accounts, gradually paying interest on the collected memories. A most valuable inheritance children are due.

Brenda remembered being extremely shy as a child. Back in the year 1976, when she was just seven years old, there was a carnival at school. Part of her wanted to attend, but her shyness was much stronger, so she decided not to go. Her grandmother, Naomi, was aware of Brenda's struggle. After much prodding, she was able to convince the young girl to attend by allowing Brenda to set one condition: After the carnival, Naomi's husband, Elimelech, would take her fishing. This was one of Brenda's favorite pastimes. They even dug worms together beforehand to solidify their agreement.

Grandma Naomi took Brenda to the carnival. When they first arrived, they purchased ten dollars' worth of tickets. Hand in hand, the pair walked through the small fair. When Brenda passed by the other children, she would briefly greet them with a smile, then look down toward the floor in embarrassment because of her need to hold her grandmother's hand for courage.

The two generations, some sixty-odd years apart, slowly walked around observing the various games the carnival offered. Brenda would watch until she knew how to play—or so she pretended. She was secretly setting her hopeful sights on the prizes, usually small stuffed animals. The young girl would wait patiently until the line was short or choose a game where there was no line at all. When it came time for her turn to play, she would quickly whisper a prayer in hopes of winning, and then she'd say a second with even more sincerity, pleading that no one would see her more than likely fail.

One by one, her tickets slowly began to disappear, but she still hadn't won a prize. The baseball toss, the dart throw, the ring toss, the basketball hoop shoot. Before each turn, Naomi would gently squeeze her granddaughter's hand in reassurance, yet she never won.

When Brenda's tickets were nearly half gone, she was finally granted victory by knocking down all three pins at the bowling game. The reward was her very own goldfish. Always looking and rarely swimming, the little fish was completely content living within its small world of water. It was contained and restrained within an average-sized clear plastic bag topped with a twist and a tie.

Having finally won something, understandably, a great deal of pressure was released from within the young girl. The much-needed and appreciated feeling of peace took its place. Still holding Naomi's hand, she gently tugged, indicating that she had something of the private nature to tell her grandmother. "I need to go pee."

When she emerged from the restroom, the girl's smile was instantly erased at the sight of the tears running down her grandmother's face. Quickly, Brenda's tears outnumbered Naomi's due to the vision of the small fish floating upside down in the plastic bag.

Needing consolation and, more importantly, unconditional love, Brenda instinctively hugged the old woman's waist. The grandmother now regretted bringing Brenda to the carnival in the first place.

In an obvious attempt at cheer, the elder reminded the younger of her fishing date with her grandfather. With the speed and simplicity of a unanimous decision of two, the pair simultaneously agreed it was time to leave.

True to form, Naomi and Brenda walked hand in hand toward the exit doors. While walking in this direction, they couldn't help but notice music coming from the direction of the doors, which gradually became louder and louder with each step they took. The duo looked to one another for answers. Finding none, they continued on until they discovered that the source of the music was coming from the last classroom on the right, just prior to the exit. They stopped and looked inside.

Written on the chalkboard were the words "Betty Crocker Cakewalk." Sitting on a table in front of the chalkboard were roughly twenty cakes. In front of an adjacent wall, the desks had all been pushed together, making room for the large circle of paper squares in the center of the room. The teacher's desk held the record player responsible for the music run by Grandmother Crocker, the woman in charge. She lifted the arm of the record player to stop the music. Next, she pulled a slip of paper from a jar and called out the number of the next lucky winner. With the playing field down to just three, two girls and one boy, the odds were, and the result was, no winner. So, she called out another, then another. On the fifth attempt, the number seven was called, which happened to match the number the boy was standing on. He smiled, revealing two missing teeth, both top-dead-center. Nonchalantly, he walked toward the table of cakes in an attempt to maintain the dignity of a young man who was soon to reach the double-digit mark in years. He claimed his prize, a two-layer cake covered in white frosting. Moments later, after exiting the classroom, its center was made known at the swipe of a finger. When the vanilla center mimicking the frosting was exposed, the smile with two missing teeth appeared once more.

The remaining two contestants, the pair of girls, whispered to one another, giggled, and then left the classroom, leaving it empty except for Grandmother Crocker. She spoke and motioned for Brenda to enter, "Come on in, sweetie. I think you are going to be today's lucky winner."

Once again, the grandmother and granddaughter looked to one another for answers, and once more, there were none to be found. They entered the classroom.

"Well, my little darling, do you happen to have any tickets left?" Inquired Mrs. Crocker. Nodding yes and pulling out her remaining tickets from the front pocket of her jeans as proof, Brenda showed them to the kind older woman.

"Perfect! That looks like just enough. How would you like to trade the rest of your tickets for my table full of cakes? I have roughly thirty minutes to return this classroom back to orderly fashion. You'd be doing me a great favor," she concluded.

Once again, Brenda and Naomi looked at one another. This time, the smiles on both of their faces indicated that the third time truly is the charm. They both knew the obvious answer.

"Yes, Ma'am. I'd like that," answered Brenda. Naomi squeezed her granddaughter's hand and then gave her "the look."

"Thank you, Ma'am," Brenda added.

Carrying one cake each, it took eight trips to the car and back for all sixteen cakes to be loaded, filling the back seat and floorboards. By their final trip, Grandma Crocker had the classroom returned to normal.

Naomi didn't have the heart to ask Brenda what she planned on doing with so many cakes because of the permanent smile displayed on the young girl's face.

Ironically, sixteen was also the number of trout that Brenda and her grandfather caught later that evening at Spanaway Lake. The fish filled their cooler, which had contained ice, pop, and sandwiches on the way there. Elimelech briefly glanced at his sleeping, still-smiling granddaughter on the way home that evening. He was successful at capturing the sight in his mind's photo album of precious memories.

Brenda spent that Saturday night at her grandparent's home. The next morning, they attended church together. When they returned home, the smell of pot roast filled their house with love and goodness. Their afternoon dinner was enjoyed on TV trays in the living room, which was not a bad thing. The kitchen table was full of cakes. No one made any inquiries or suggestions to Brenda about what she planned to do with the cakes. They just were.

As the following day at school was about to end, Brenda's teacher, Mrs. Damon, made an announcement, "Well, class, we are going to have a party this Friday. As you all know, this year is the Bicentennial celebration of our country, which means she is two hundred years old. An extremely long time in people years, but very young in terms of a country. Anyway, I need some volunteers; some need to help make decorations, others need to help sort costumes from the school's storage room in the basement. I need help with refreshments, both things to eat and drink. Okay, guys, please tell me how you'd like to help."

As usual, Lisa was the first to raise her hand.

"Yes, Lisa," the teacher said.

"I'll bring my fruit punch," the girl offered.

One by one came the other volunteers.

"I'll help with the decorations."

"Can I help sort costumes?"

"Me too."

"I'll bring some potato chips."

"I'll bring the dip."

Brenda also wanted to offer to help, but her shyness kept her hand glued to the desk. However, when the bell rang, indicating the school day was over, she stopped for a moment at the teacher's desk and softly informed her of her intention.

That Friday, Naomi drove Brenda to school. During the first half of the day, Mrs. Damon's lessons included math, reading, and social studies. After lunch, the afternoon was mainly a lesson on history as the students readied for the Bicentennial Celebration. Colorful decorations were placed, and chairs were lined up. The record player was positioned with records sitting next to it, which were placed in the order to be played. The refreshments were set out. When it was time for the party to begin, one by one, the classes entered the gym and took their places.

The principal began the celebration with a prayer—back in the day when this was still allowed. The afternoon celebration was highlighted by the school play that included skits and performances portraying important events such as The Boston Tea Party, The Signing of The Declaration of Independence, Paul Revere's Ride, The Winter at Valley Forge, and the deciding battle of the war, The Battle of Saratoga. The play ended with square dancing by those dressed in costumes of the era.

Next, the refreshments were served as all of the students mingled and visited with each other. When it was time to wind things down, the principal instructed the students to return to their seats for the final highlight of the day's celebration.

Next, he led the assembly in song. "Happy birthday to you, happy birthday to you. Happy birthday, dear America. Happy birthday to you!"

Catching the spirit of freedom and the camaraderie of the moment, the students all rose to their feet and then began again, "Happy birthday to you, happy birthday to you . . ."

One by one, each row of children walked to the front of the gymnasium. Directly in front of the American flag hanging on the wall was Brenda's table full of cakes, having turned into those of the birthday variety. Side by side, the young girl and grandmother handed each student a slice, which were happily received.

"Thanks, Brenda."

"Boy, it looks good."

"Chocolate is my favorite!"

"I like vanilla. Is there any?"

"Dang, Brenda. Good job!"

"Brenda, did you make all these?"

"You got the coolest grandma ever."

"Thanks, Brenda."

After all of the students returned to their seats, there was just one cake left, German chocolate, which happened to be both Brenda's and her grandmother's favorite. Smiling, once again, they both looked at one another, this time not in search of answers, just with knowing looks.

Brenda was jolted back to the present by her children's laughter. Still smiling, she entered the yard once more, pleased to have taken the time to observe, appreciate, and reflect. She walked to the flowerbeds and complimented her children on their work.

Soon, the side gate opened, drawing their attention. Just arriving home from work, Father entered the yard and said, "Hey, guys!"

"Dad, Dad," greeted the sister and brother at almost the same time. The kids were very happy to have Trevor at home. They gave him hugs; Jojo hugged him around the waist, and Hudson hugged his leg.

Still holding onto her father, Jojo declared, "Dad, we saw the police and a bank robber today. Well, not really a bank robber. I don't think, anyway."

Trevor replied, "You're right, Jojo. He wasn't. I heard about the incident from your mother, then again on the radio on the way home from work today. The man that you saw had just finished quarantining from Covid. He was wearing his mask because he didn't want to chance exposing anyone. He had pulled into the bank parking lot and then realized he had forgotten his wallet. He didn't even get out of his car. When he was on his way back home to get his wallet, he was pulled over by the police because the bank did happen to get robbed at about the same time he was there. When he didn't have any ID when he got stopped, it made the police more suspicious. It turns out it was a Korean man who robbed the bank. He had a yellow car with no bumper stickers, by the way. So, thankfully, both men are where they belong tonight. The black man is home with his family, and the real bank robber, the Korean man, is in jail."

Jojo smiled, then said, "I'm so glad."

Trevor replied, "You guys had quite a morning and then a busy afternoon in the yard. What do you say we play until supper?"

"Sure, we just finished," Jojo replied. Answering by action, Hudson went to the swing set and motioned for his dad to come push him.

Brenda also welcomed her husband, saying, "I'm so glad you're home, Trevor," then gave him a light kiss on the cheek. She spoke again, "I'd better go keep an eye on dinner. Honey, do you got this?" She smiled and nodded toward the kids.

"No place I'd rather be," Trevor responded, also smiling as he followed Hudson toward the swings.

Jojo walked to the tree containing the tree fort and began to climb. A rope and ladder were two other ways to gain entrance, but Jojo preferred climbing the branches.

Trevor began pushing Hudson on the swing set. Hudson let out a gleeful "Weee, weee" each time he rose higher off the ground.

Trevor experienced a tired but complete feeling every day when he reunited with his children after work.

Jojo, now in the tree fort, began looking out of its windows, which gave her a vantage point of her yard and others in the neighborhood. Just beyond their fence, she noticed an old woman in a wheelchair enjoying her backyard as well. Jojo studied the lady and wondered why she had never seen her before.

CHAPTER SIX

A middle-aged couple without children named the Simons lived next door. Jojo assumed the old woman must be a guest and continued to watch her. The Simons were good neighbors. Her father had talked about them before, mentioning that they were quiet and kept their home maintained in a fashion he wished all neighbors did. Jojo agreed that the Simons were good people. She thought Mrs. Simons was a standup lady because she decorated her yard for every major holiday, making it a very friendly place for children. These neighbors always smiled and waved, even just in passing. Proving true that people's actions often speak much more clearly than mere words do.

Jojo noticed that the older woman seemed happy, moving slowly around in her wheelchair as she stopped to admire the different plants and a birdbath that decorated the yard. Something inside told Jojo she must meet the woman.

Using the rope, the fastest means of exiting the tree fort, she climbed down. Once on the ground, she went to Father and asked permission to go meet the woman.

Trevor was still pushing his son back and forth when Jojo said, "Dad, there's an older woman next door at the Simons'. I've never seen her before. I feel bad for her. She's in a wheelchair. Can I go meet her? Please?"

"I'll tell you what, Jo, I'll introduce you over the fence, and if she says it's okay, then you can go meet her after dinner. She is Mrs. Simons' mother, named Ruby, by the way. She is going to spend the summer. I met her myself this morning on the way to work. She seems nice," answered Father.

Trevor brought Hudson's swing to a stop, and the young boy made a pouty face. To switch his son's attention from the swing to the neighbor, Trevor pointed to the fence and stated, "Meet the neighbor." Hudson's sour look turned into one of wonder.

Jojo was already waiting by the fence when Father arrived, holding Hudson's hand. Jojo jumped up and down at the fence's edge. She could see the old woman for a split second each time her face cleared the top of the fence, then quickly disappeared from sight on the way back down. Father held Hudson on his shoulder, ready to introduce his son and bouncing daughter to the lady confined to the wheelchair.

As soon as he saw the woman, Hudson held out his arms, exclaiming, "Gamma, gamma."

"Hi, Ruby," Trevor greeted the woman. "I want to introduce my pride, Jojo," pointing to his daughter, who rose above the fence and disappeared just as quickly, "And my joy, Hudson," he finished lifting his son a fraction higher.

"I am very pleased to meet the both of you," Ruby told the Cobbler children.

"Would it be okay if Jojo came over after dinner for a visit? She would very much like to meet you," Trevor asked.

"Of course, she can. I look forward to it. How about next time you come too, Hudson? Okay? And please do call me Grandma. I would be honored."

Having officially met Ruby, the Cobblers turned back to face their own yard. So, it was agreed; Jojo would go next door and meet Ruby after dinner.

"Weee, weee," Hudson cheered, once again being pushed on the swing by Father, up and down, up and down. Jojo climbed back up to the tree fort to watch the old woman she now knew as Ruby, who, out of the corner of her eye, noticed she was being watched from above. Both the young girl in the tree fort and the woman in the wheelchair smiled to themselves at the same time, each looking forward to their visit.

Soon after Father and the kids resumed play, Brenda began to bring dinner to the picnic table. Eyeing Mother carrying the food, Jojo quickly climbed down from the tree fort. Neither Father nor Hudson needed to be called for dinner either.

Eating dinner outside at the picnic table was a special treat. The family hungrily ate a meal of fried chicken, pork-n-beans, potato chips, and green salad. For dessert, they had chocolate pudding.

As soon as she was finished eating supper, Jojo asked, "Mom, Dad, can I go visit Ruby now?"

"First, help me carry in the dishes and change out of those dirty clothes, then you can go, kiddo," Mother answered.

Mother and Jojo brought the dirty dishes into the kitchen. They sat them in the sink, which was beginning to fill with hot water and dish soap. Bubbles formed in the dish soap. Smaller ones, colored white and clear, stayed near the top of the water and clung to the dishes. Larger bubbles rose when they began to expand. Shades of red and blue could be seen in them just before they popped. Mother gave Jojo permission to go next door to the Simons as soon as she changed her clothes, which she did in record time.

CHAPTER SEVEN

Jojo stood in front of the Simons' home. The front door was open, but the screen door was shut. The smell of dinner drifted past Jojo as she rang the doorbell. The unmistakable aroma of broccoli and some type of casserole greeted the girl before Mrs. Simons did. Jojo thought how thankful she was to be coming over *after* dinner and not *for* dinner. Jojo hated broccoli.

Mrs. Simons answered the door, "Jojo, come on in. I heard you were coming over. Ruby is looking forward to your company. Can I get you something to eat?"

"No, thanks. I already ate," answered Jojo, truthfully and thankfully. She thought to herself, *Maybe it's better they don't have children if this is how they eat*, then smiled.

Mrs. Simons' first name was Lorraine. At forty-six years old, she was a little on the thin side with attractive features. Her hair was nearly all golden in color, with just a few gradual exceptions of strands of gray here and there. The lines in the upward direction near the corners of her eyes revealed that her smiles greatly outnumbered the frowns during her life. She led Jojo into the kitchen. Mr. Simons was occupied reading a newspaper at the table. Only his hands and the top of his head were visible.

"Mom's out back," Mrs. Simons told Jojo.

"Hi, neighbor," Mr. Simons said without leaving the cover of his paper.

"Hello," Jojo replied as she went out the back door, happy to get away from the broccoli smell. She was even happier to see the smiling woman in the wheelchair.

"Hi, my little friend," welcomed Ruby, "one sec," she paused, made a puffy face, then burped quietly, her hand covering her mouth.

"Excuse me, dang broccoli gives me gas something awful," she informed Jojo. Jojo began to laugh. She had a tough time stopping. Ruby laughed, too, and the ice was broken.

Seeds of friendship began to sprout between the old woman bound to her wheelchair, entering the winter of her life, and the young girl, whose life was beginning to blossom from her own, early spring's sun.

Ruby motioned with her head for Jojo to follow. The older woman's hands gripped the wheels of her chair. She moved herself away from the house toward a small area of flowers that surrounded the birdbath. The wheels of the wheelchair left an imprint on the grass that Jojo noticed as she followed.

A tree stood to the left. Only a portion of the birdbath and flowers were still receiving sunlight as the evening began to advance. The majority rested in the shadows.

Ruby stopped the wheelchair in the light of the sun to feel its warmth and began to speak, "My son-in-law, Darryl, uhm, Mr. Simons, made this area for me. It doesn't seem like much, but to an old lady like me, it makes my visit more comfortable. My own space, you could say. You see, I have a fondness for birds. I became fascinated with them when I was younger. Younger than you. It seems like such a long time ago. Which, of course, it was . . ."

Her voice began to taper off. She started to remember the past. She told Jojo many things, and Jojo listened and learned. She learned about Ruby and her life. Ruby told her about Lost Lake, the eagle, and her friend, the baby snow goose. Immediately, Jojo felt a connection with Ruby. A common love for birds and a gentle magnetic draw. She learned about other things, too. Special things. Important things.

As a child, Ruby once read that birds are almost angelic. The nearest things we have on Earth to the angels in Heaven. When Ruby spoke, Jojo listened and learned. Ruby told her stories. Ruby explained that birds in flight come closer to Heaven than any other being. Maybe, just maybe, sometimes they come so close they can hear the music there. The music of angels. Ruby wondered if that's where birds got their songs from.

Ruby had neat ideas. She was smart. When she spoke, her eyes would twinkle and shine. Ruby didn't look old when she spoke of these things. It was easy to see Ruby had been pretty when she was young. Her eyes were still pretty. Her eyes were still young.

Jojo understood Ruby. Some of the things she already knew. Sometimes, before Ruby finished a sentence, Jojo knew what was going to be said. Jojo knew. Ruby knew. Things that were of the secret type, they could both now share with each other. For now.

Ruby had been outside in her yard early that morning when Jojo fed the morning birds. She had been in the yard, but she couldn't see Jojo in her yard because of her wheelchair and the fence. She heard the birds and saw them leave. She saw worms in some of their beaks. Then she saw Jojo at her window. She watched Jojo watch the birds. Ruby was like Jojo, only older. Jojo was like Ruby.

Jojo didn't see her morning birds turn and land in the tree near the birdbath. Jojo didn't see Ruby speaking to the birds. Sometimes when Ruby thought, she spoke to birds. They would come. She could also speak to other animals when she tried. When she thought to.

When Ruby was younger, she wanted to know more. She studied music in college. Peaceful, happy music. Ruby also learned to fly. Something inside told her that she had to. Her days in college were split: half learning and playing music and the other half learning to fly airplanes. When she could, she flew by herself. She flew very high.

Ruby desired to see Heaven, just a glimpse. Sometimes she would fly so high the airplane ran poorly, and it made bad sounds. The air was too thin. Then one day, it happened; the plane quit running. It would not start. She thought the doors to Heaven were either closed or hidden from her. They were not. She was just looking the wrong way.

The plane began to go down. It refused to start. Before the plane crashed, Ruby felt peace, and she found the way to Heaven, too. The secret she discovered was that you must believe.

When the plane was going down very fast, Ruby leaped from it wearing her parachute. It was too late to land safely. The plane crashed and caught fire. Ruby landed with her parachute, but it hadn't opened properly. She landed very hard. Ruby broke her back and was paralyzed. She lost the use of her legs but found peace.

Ruby's story seemed to pause. Complete darkness had gradually arrived, almost unnoticed by either of them.

"You are going to have to go home now, child. We don't want to start summer off by getting your parents to worrying none. Before you leave, though,

I have one more thing to share. Something for you to think about. You are very special. You share the light. You have gifts inside. Some you realize, some you don't. I'm so glad we met. Some things are supposed to happen. I believe our meeting is one. Destiny is a perfect word for it. It's quite possible our meeting, our friendship, will be an important part of each of our destinies," Ruby concluded.

Surprised, Jojo opened her mouth to respond, but before she could ask any questions, Lorraine turned on an outside light above the back door, opened it, and informed them that Brenda had phoned and said it was time for Jojo to go home.

"She was just getting ready to go. We lost track of time," Ruby explained. Jojo and Ruby exchanged goodbyes.

In bed that night, after saying her prayers, Jojo thought about what Ruby had told her. She thought about how scary the plane crash must have been. She also considered how Ruby seemed happy even though she couldn't walk. Ruby had told Jojo about destiny and about sharing the light. These words kept repeating themselves in Jojo's mind. Jojo understood, but just partly. She wished she knew exactly what Ruby meant about sharing the light, though, and she wanted to know more about the definition of destiny.

Jojo was sure happy that Ruby was spending the summer next door. She kept thinking and wondering, reflecting on the conversation they just shared.

CHAPTER EIGHT

After a while, the old owl landed in his tree. He announced his visit like always with a "Who, who, whooo." His introduction quieted Jojo's thoughts. She got out of bed and went to the window.

"Are you ready?" The owl asked.

Jojo's mouth opened in surprise.

"Ready?" Jojo inquired in a tone of uncertainty. Then, she thought she might have imagined it.

"Ruby is waiting for you. She told me to tell you to meet her in her front yard," the owl said again.

"You can speak?" Jojo asked in disbelief.

"Of course, more than just a 'who,' that's for sure," answered the owl.

"How come you've never said anything to me before?" Jojo asked.

"There was never a need. More than likely, if I had, you wouldn't have heard me anyway. You weren't quite ready yet. Ruby told me you are ready now. She also told me to tell you she's waiting," instructed the owl.

"My parents would totally freak out if I went next door this late!" Jojo exclaimed.

"Ruby expected such an answer. You are a well-behaved child living in a home filled with love. Ruby suggested you ask your parents if it's okay," advised the owl.

"Are you crazy?" snapped Jojo. "My parents are in bed. There's no way that—" she was cut off.

"It's okay, child. Go ask your parents. I'm waiting for you." Now, Ruby seemed to have spoken to her through the owl, who slowly nodded his head as if giving his approval and then flew away.

Jojo thought to herself, *Maybe I'm crazy.*

"Come, Jojo. Trust. Believe." Now, Ruby somehow spoke to her without the owl. Her voice rang in Jojo's head instead.

"I'll ask . . . I guess," Jojo answered.

She had mixed feelings at this point. She knew her parents were probably asleep. There was no way she'd wake them up. There was no way they'd let her go, but something inside told her to try. That it would be okay.

Her parent's door was slightly ajar. Jojo peered in. Her father was asleep, and Mother was reading a book.

"Mom," she whispered. Brenda sat her book down and put a finger to her lips to signal Jojo to be quiet. She waved her daughter to her side of the bed. Jojo went to her mother and asked quietly if she could go next door and told her that Ruby had asked her over.

"Sure, kiddo. Try not to be long, though. It's late; you need your sleep," Brenda approved. Jojo was taken by surprise.

"Are you sure?" she asked, hardly believing what she had just been told.

"Yes, I'm sure. It must be important, or Ruby wouldn't have asked, given the time of night. Go ahead, but like I said, don't be long," Brenda said.

Jojo hugged her mom and whispered, "Thanks," in her ear. *Wow*, she thought. She went to her room and changed out of her pajamas and into some cut-off jeans and a T-shirt. While getting dressed, she thought it strange that Mother didn't ask how Ruby had contacted her so late at night. While selecting tennis shoes and a coat, she dismissed the thought.

Jojo left her house thinking, *What a strange night!* Sure enough, Ruby was in her front yard waiting in her wheelchair, surrounded by a circle of light from a streetlamp on a nearby telephone pole.

"I'm glad you came," Ruby said. She winked at Jojo, then continued, "We should be on our way. I know you have questions. I'll explain in a bit. Most anyway."

She moved herself to a van sitting in the driveway. Using a remote, she opened a side door of the van. Then, a metal ramp was lowered to the ground. She pushed herself onto the ramp and then began to raise the ramp using the remote.

"Hop in, Jojo," Ruby said, pointing to the passenger front door. "It takes me a sec, but I'm almost ready." She finished. The ramp stopped moving when it was level with the floor of the van.

Jojo opened the van door and got in. She turned to face Ruby. She had never been around someone in a wheelchair before. Ruby drew the ramp in and closed the door, finished with the remote. She turned the driver's seat around to face her. Using some overhead grips, Ruby lifted herself from the wheelchair and sat down in the driver's seat. She spun around, now facing forward.

"Looks like a pain in the butt, I'm sure. I'm used to it, though. Beats having to rely on someone to drive me," Ruby explained. Jojo was impressed.

85

Ruby put the key in the ignition and started the van. A light came on when the ignition started. Jojo saw chrome levers just below the steering wheel. The light went off. Orange gauges lit up the dash. Ruby turned the heater on.

"I had this van specially made for me. I can drive as well, if not better than most drivers on the road. Not to brag. Just to hopefully comfort you some," Ruby chuckled.

Jojo couldn't contain herself anymore. She began to speak, "The owl spoke to me. You spoke to me, but you were here. How?"

Ruby replied, "I'll explain real soon. Your parents gave you permission, I take it?"

"Mom did. Dad was asleep," Jojo answered.

"Good, real good. I ask you, Jojo, I know we just met, but do you feel you can trust me?" Ruby asked.

"Yes, I do," answered Jojo honestly, "I almost feel like I have known you a long time. I just have questions, I guess. But you know what?"

"What's that, child?" Ruby asked.

"I'm real excited. We are just sitting in your van in the driveway, but I feel like I'm on an adventure or something. It feels good. It's, like, I can't wait, but I don't know what for," Jojo replied.

Ruby spoke, "Who knows? Maybe this will be an adventure of sorts. Why don't we go find out? Why don't you put on your seat belt, and we'll be on our way?"

CHAPTER NINE

Ruby and Jojo pulled out of the driveway and into the night. As they began to drive, Ruby declared, "I'm going to do some talking. It may sound like I'm long-winded, and I suppose I am at times. Let me tell you . . . You know how computers are everywhere nowadays?"

Jojo nodded.

"Every word typed, or website visited, every email sent or received is stored inside the computer, or cell phone if that's what's used. Nothing is ever

forgotten. Those who know how can discover everywhere the user has been or what they have said. To be
honest, I think it's a bunch of hogwash. There's no
such thing as privacy anymore. AI hears everything
you say and makes suggestions you don't want. It's
too much! Touchy subject for me, I guess. Anyway,
our minds are much more sophisticated than computers. What I'm getting at is: Everything that I tell
you tonight, you will remember when you need to. If
it seems like I'm rambling, please be patient and bear
with me. There are reasons."

Ruby talked as she drove. She drove safely as she
spoke, but her mind was seemingly somewhere else.
It was the same for Jojo. She looked straight ahead,
out of the windshield, but her mind was focused on
Ruby's words. Her eyes saw the road, but her mind
saw what Ruby meant.

As Jojo listened closely to Ruby, butterflies flut-
tered in her stomach, anticipating the unknown that
she somehow knew would be important.

The van drove with no apparent destination, yet
Ruby's words were going exactly where they were
supposed to, inside of Jojo. Like earlier in the evening,

in the yard, Ruby spoke of many things. When she spoke, Jojo could often relate and always understand.

Ruby explained that scientists claim the hardest thing on earth is the diamond. She said they are mistaken. The human heart and mind can be much harder and more valuable, for that matter. She said that scientists could take a chalkboard and put a bunch of letters, numbers, and fancy symbols on it to prove different. In a way, they are right. But in many ways, they're wrong, she felt. Likewise, inside, deep inside, our minds and our hearts are the same way. Again, scientists can and will prove they are two separate organs. Ruby believed that this was physically true but spiritually wrong.

"Jojo, the best thing that ever happened to me was my plane crash. Sounds crazy, but I mean it. I lost the use of my legs but gained a strong understanding of my mind. Sometimes, people who have disabling accidents overcome by becoming stronger in other aspects. This was true for me. For example, my accident opened my communication with the birds and more. Like the owl speaking to you last night, and after that, when I spoke to you through the owl, then after he flew off. Almost everyone is capable of communicating with nature by developing unique, undiscovered powers within themselves. But sadly, very, very few know how. If they only knew where and when to look. You share the light, Jojo. That means you have the key to be able to speak in ways others can't, to and through animals, for example, and to other people who are far away, even those in Heaven. The key to knowing people's thoughts and to knowing some things before they happen. I will show you how to use your light. How to use your key," Ruby paused, allowing her words to sink in.

Jojo slowly considered what she had just been told. She had often felt there was a greater communication to be had, but she was never quite able to put her finger on it. After hearing what Ruby had just said, she smiled to herself, now knowing that it was possible. She was eager to learn more. However, Ruby changed her tone as she spoke, "One more quick thing. God doesn't make mistakes. He came close, though, when he made those dang crows. Dang blackbirds, most selfish, useless, annoying . . . I'll have to explain later." She stopped talking as they pulled into a convenience store parking lot.

"Jojo, I'm getting a little hungry and thirsty. How about you?" Ruby asked.

"I sure am," Jojo replied, then she continued, "Some cocoa sounds good, and I could use something to eat. I'm a little hungry too."

"Anything you want, child. I'm craving some nachos myself, soaked in cheese, topped with jalapenos. Probably wash it down with a Dr. Pepper. I have an idea! Kind of a game of sorts . . . When we're in the store, don't tell me what you want to get. I know about the cocoa, but that's it. Look at things. Fool me with your eyes. Tell me with your mind. Think about what you want, but don't say it. Okay?"

"Got it!" Jojo exclaimed. She shivered from excitement. Her heart felt like it was pounding like a drum. She couldn't wait to try.

"One last instruction. I know I said anything you want, but I am an old woman trying to make my money last. Don't break me in there," laughed Ruby. Jojo laughed, too.

While Ruby was getting herself out of the side door, Jojo was thinking to herself how she was glad to have met Ruby. She already thought of the old woman as her friend, possibly even her best friend.

"Bet you never would have thought your best friend would be an eccentric old woman in a wheelchair, huh?" Ruby asked knowingly.

It had already begun.

The store clerk offered to help with Ruby's order out of kindness and respect. Sure enough, Ruby had the clerk make her a large order of nachos topped with cheese and jalapenos.

"A Big Gulp Dr. Pepper, no ice. I'm not paying good money for frozen water, I tell you." Ruby completed her order. The clerk and Jojo both smiled. *This lady's awesome*, Jojo thought. Ruby knew Jojo's thought. She smiled to herself but didn't say anything about it.

Jojo was kind of nervous at the idea that Ruby could tell what she was thinking. She thought she might make a mistake somehow. Maybe she'd just tell Ruby that she was right, even if she was wrong about what Jojo chose to eat.

"Old age guarantees gray hair and wrinkles. Tummy aches often come by choice. So don't worry. Relax, and don't humor me. True friends have no secrets. Lies cannot exist in communication like ours," Ruby said.

To no surprise, Ruby was correct at guessing Jojo's mouth's and stomach's desires. A box of raspberry-filled powdered donuts, a Big Grab of Cheetos, and two packs of string cheese, plus her cocoa. What Jojo thought, Ruby said. In the line, while the clerk was ringing up the purchases, Jojo thought she should have gotten some water.

"Jojo, why don't you grab us a couple of Dasanis?" Ruby suggested. Jojo was amazed and also a little nervous knowing that someone could read her thoughts. She quickly tried to remember if she had ever thought about something weird or possibly embarrassing around Ruby.

"You are too young and innocent to have anything but a clear conscience, child. So once again, please don't worry," Ruby reassured her.

They left the convenience store. Ruby rested her Dr. Pepper between her legs. Once in a while, she would raise it to her mouth and sip from a straw. Jojo sipped her cocoa and ate a donut. Powdered sugar stuck to her lips and the corners of her mouth. She tried to wipe it away with her tongue between bites. Jojo ate another donut and then finished her cocoa.

While Ruby drove, she spoke, "Jojo, tonight I'm going to make you aware of some things. Like I said earlier, when you need to, you'll remember them. For some reason, just after Christmas, I had an urge to spend the summer with my daughter, Lorraine, and son-in-law, Darryl. Shortly after the New Year, I phoned them and basically invited myself. Ordinarily, I am not one to want to stray from home. I am a very private person. I enjoy being by myself. Don't get me wrong; I love people. Good Lord knows that, but if given a choice, I'd prefer being alone to a crowd any day. For me to have an internal tugging to want to spend three months sharing a home, even with my daughter, I knew it had to be important. After meeting you, I felt you were the reason for my conscience telling me to spend the summer next door to you."

CHAPTER TEN

The van came to a stop at the front entrance of Wapato Lake Park. A chain blocking the entrance with a red stop sign in the center denied their passage. A green sign with reflective letters explained that the park was open daily from dawn until dusk.

"Just as well," Ruby said. "We'll park on the hill overlooking the lake. I'm starving, and my nachos are getting cold. It's definitely time to stop."

Jojo knew the park well. Her family had enjoyed picnics there quite a few times. A roped-off section of the lake contained a swimming area with a slide. She had swum there with her mother during many of these visits while Father and Hudson barbecued.

Ruby brought the van to rest at the end of a dirt road. Directly in front of them, the moon lit up the lake; its reflection was mirrored on the water. The edge of the lake could easily be made out. When Jojo's eyes left the view of the water, things couldn't be seen clearly anymore. The outline of some trees could be distinguished if they were tall enough. Shorter ones blended in with bushes. It was too dark to clearly see anything beyond the water, and it had to be accepted that way.

Ruby began eating her nachos, which had become soggy due to the melted cheese, the juice from the jalapenos, and time. She didn't mind. Jojo drank from one of the bottled waters. She had become thirsty from her sugary food and drink. Part way through, after putting her thirst at bay, she capped the water and set it down. Soon, Ruby finished her nachos. She licked her fingers thoroughly, getting all of the cheese flavor she could. Then, she wiped them on a couple of napkins, which she wadded up and, without looking, tossed backward over her shoulder to the rear of the van, because it was her van and she could if she wanted to.

Jojo and Ruby watched a single swan float across the lake. Neither one said a word. It passed through the moon's reflection on the water, disturbing it temporarily. After a while, the swan was not visible anymore. Small ripples on the lake, telling of its way, eventually vanished. The moon's reflection was once again granted peace and its entirety.

Jojo thought to herself. So did Ruby. They both spoke at the same time, cutting one another off.

"Jinx," Ruby said.

"You owe me a soda," said Jojo. They laughed together.

"You go first," Jojo offered.

"No, child. I believe it's age before beauty," Ruby answered, smiling. Her eyes twinkled. Her face seemed to glow. Jojo could see her face more clearly now. More clearly than moments before, for some reason.

Jojo began, "I have a lot of fun here with my family. We play frisbee. We barbecue. We go swimming. We really love it here, but just a few minutes ago, when you and I were not saying anything and just watching the swan float across the water, I felt happier than I've ever felt here before."

From the mouth of babes, Ruby thought.

"My mom has said that before, usually after I've said something that surprised or shocked her. I'm not exactly sure what it means, though," Jojo commented. She didn't realize that Ruby hadn't spoken aloud. Jojo had read her mind. Ruby noticed but didn't say anything. Ruby now knew, without a doubt, that she had been correct in choosing Jojo. This had been no mistake.

"Let's play a game of sorts, Jojo," Ruby suggested.

"Sure, anything, anything at all," agreed Jojo.

"I want you to think of the swan floating across the water again. Picture it in your mind exactly how it looked from when you first saw it until just when it disappeared from sight, every detail. I'm going to do it with you. K? Close your eyes and see. And if you don't mind, can I hold your hand while we do it?" Ruby asked.

"Sure," answered Jojo. They held hands.

"Together, let's close our eyes," Ruby continued.

Now! Ruby mentally instructed the swan.

Jojo's eyes were closed. She saw the lake. She didn't see the swan. The eyes of her mind searched for it in the shadows, where it had emerged from before. Still no sight of it. While the two held hands, Ruby's grip became slightly firmer. Now, Jojo saw the swan. It floated across the lake just like before, and as before, neither Jojo nor Ruby spoke.

When the swan was about to disappear from sight, Ruby spoke, "Keep your eyes closed, child, and watch."

Jojo's eyes remained shut. She saw the swan floating into the darkness. She could see the swan, but she couldn't tell where the water ended and the darkness began. They continued holding hands with their eyes closed. Watching.

Power from Ruby's touch made Jojo see more clearly with her thoughts. When Ruby gripped her hand tighter, the power increased, feeling kind of like the slight spark you sometimes get when you touch someone after walking across new carpet. Jojo also had the power. She just didn't know how to use it yet. Ruby was going to show her how. It was inside Jojo behind a door that she had never opened before. The door protected an area of special secrets and abilities. Jojo's inner light was the key to the door. Tonight, Ruby was going to help her unlock and use her own special powers. The right way, for the right reasons—to help others.

"Come!" Ruby beckoned. Jojo knew Ruby hadn't meant her. As the swan began to rise, it gradually started to emerge from the darkness. Jojo could tell it had just left the lake because silvery drops of water were cast aside when it shook itself off.

Briefly, Jojo opened her eyes and glanced at Ruby. Ruby's eyes were still closed. Her face was glowing more than before. She looked younger. She looked happy. Ruby knew Jojo was looking at her.

With her eyes still shut, she turned toward Jojo and smiled. Jojo knew that Ruby knew her eyes were open. She also knew that Ruby could see with her eyes closed. As soon as Jojo closed her eyes again, the swan reappeared. She could tell it was coming toward them, toward Ruby's voice, toward Ruby's glowing face.

The swan kept coming. It stopped when it was right in front of them. Ruby said, "Let's open our eyes at the same time. K? On three. One, two, three."

They opened their eyes. The beautiful swan was resting on Ruby's hood, completely at peace, just like it would be sitting on a nest of eggs. It was the same either way, eyes open or shut.

"Wow. That was so cool. Do you think you could show me how? I mean, do you think I could?" Jojo asked.

Ruby answered, "I don't *think* you can. I *know* you can, but our hands are getting sweaty. Let's give it a break."

As soon as they let go, they dried their palms. Ruby wiped hers on her pants, and Jojo dried hers on her cut-offs. The swan stayed on the hood of the van, perfectly content to rest and wait for Ruby's next instruction.

"We'll get back to the swan shortly. Do me a favor, Jojo, pull down your visor," Ruby stated. Jojo reached forward and lowered the visor on her side of the windshield. It revealed a mirror. Jojo saw herself in the mirror.

"Keep looking at yourself," Ruby said. She took her hand and lightly touched the girl's shoulder. At the exact moment Ruby touched her, Jojo watched her own face glow brightly in the mirror. She smiled, which made her glow even more. Ruby removed her hand. Jojo's face still glowed a little, but not as much as before.

"Oh, my gosh, Ruby!" Jojo exclaimed. "I can't believe it. You're magic, huh?"

"In a way, I guess you could say. Now we'll switch. The proverbial shoe on the other's foot . . . I mean, it's your turn. Look at me, Jojo," Ruby answered and instructed. Jojo watched as Ruby held out her hand and motioned for Jojo to take it. When she put her hand into Ruby's, Ruby's face lit up. She removed it. Ruby's face wasn't as bright.

"Put it back and squeeze, child," Ruby told Jojo. Again, Jojo placed her hand in Ruby's. As soon as she touched her, Ruby's face glowed more.

"Hard as you can. You won't hurt me," Ruby stated. The harder Jojo squeezed, the brighter Ruby's face became.

Jojo was using her own power now.

"Jojo, I'm going to be quiet for a bit. I want the things that have happened tonight to sink in. I'd like you to reflect on them. You have just shown both of us that magic lives in you. Neat, huh?" Ruby said with a smile.

"Yeah. Oh, yeah. It's hard to believe that I could make your face light up. I am so happy. No—more than that. I don't know exactly how to say it. I'm, like, way past happy. I mean, ever since I was little, I've felt different. A little different than most people. Then, I thought that I must be wrong. Everyone probably felt that way. I thought it was normal to feel different. I thought . . ." Jojo paused. She stared at the lake.

Ruby whispered, "That's right, child. That's right. Don't speak."

Time went by. Then, it stopped. For exactly how long, unknown, or had it even stopped? Recognizing the pause, Jojo's mind took her by the hand and led her through trails of the past. Every once in a while, she stopped and visited a memory. She noticed things. Many of the past memories that seemed confusing at the time, she now understood as lessons. Some of them, anyway. She saw times when she had used her power, like the time her father had misplaced his car keys. She didn't know where they were, but some-how, she knew where to look, and sure enough, she found them. She didn't know how she'd known at the time, but she had done it. Answers started coming to Jojo. More answers than questions, which had once been ignored. She just needed to ask more. Answers could not exist without questions coming first. It had to equal out. She was only eleven years old. She did her best to find balance and understanding. She tried so hard, but she couldn't.

Jojo began to cry. It was too much. Ruby began to cry, too. Ruby understood. Ruby remembered how tough things had been for her at first. Ruby felt bad for Jojo. She felt happy for her, too, because she knew.

Ruby pulled Jojo close and hugged her. Ruby had seen glimpses of Jojo's life ahead. She knew she would be okay. She knew Jojo would be happy and that they would always be together. Ruby also knew that she didn't have much time. The night would soon be over. She had to continue to teach. Ruby hugged Jojo a little harder. She wiped Jojo's tears and nose on her coat. She didn't care about her coat. She cared about Jojo. She loved Jojo. Ruby gradually released the hug. She took her hand and pushed Jojo's hair back. She smiled at Jojo. Jojo smiled back. Jojo became more at ease. She understood it was important. The stress of the unknown passed. She was back in the present. It was now, and now it was okay.

Jojo took a drink of water. She sat back in her seat. She waited. She knew. Ruby knew, too. Ruby began to speak, "As a man thinketh, so is he. That means we become what we think about. Good or bad. Our thoughts can hurt us or help us. Our thoughts decide our actions, which pave the way to our destiny. Jojo, magic is inside most everyone. Hardly anyone knows this, let alone how to use it. I believe you carry very, very strong magic. That doesn't mean anything spooky or negative, if it is used properly. Good things in the hands of bad people always turn bad. It's the way it is. Kind of an unwritten rule. The opposite is also true. Good in the hands of good becomes great, and miracles happen. I saw light coming from you when I first met you. Every time you jumped above the fence to look at me, I saw light rise with you. I could even see it during the day. Earlier tonight, when we first visited in my backyard, do you remember when it became dark out, but we kept talking? We could still see each other because we shared our light. Your face glowed. So did mine. Together. You didn't notice it then. Most people will never see it. That's why no one noticed it in you before. I saw it right away.

"Always remember. The light is light. It is also the key. It is also a power. Like magic, which is past the key, but the same as the light. I know it sounds confusing. You WILL see and remember. You will know. Each is its own, but also part of the whole. I wish I could explain more, but there isn't going to be enough time.

"Jojo, I have come as far as I can. I'm proud of my life's accomplishments. I can honestly say the world is a better place. I am not done, though.

Now, I am as good as YOU become. That's what I call 'bettering of the soul.' Every parent's ultimate goal is for their children to become more successful in life than they were. For their life to become easier. When people have special powers, it is even more important to pass them on, to show others who are blessed how to use the powers to take further steps. Not just for the sake of the ones who pass it on or those who receive the powers. It is vital for all who have, or ever will experience life on Earth. It's a responsibility. Small deeds produce large results." She paused. "What do you say we let him go?" Ruby nodded toward the swan, still resting on the hood as if it were the most natural thing on Earth for him to do.

"I'm sure he'd like that. He's probably getting bored, huh?" Jojo answered.

"Go ahead. Send him away, child. Think where you want him to go. He will obey. He wants to. He has to. Trust and understanding occurred in the beginning with Adam when God gave him the honor of naming all the animals. Even more so a while later when God gave Noah the responsibility of keeping all the species of animals alive on his arc during the great flood that covered the entire earth," Ruby told her.

"Should I tell him to swim back across the lake?" Jojo asked quietly. For some reason, she felt kind of embarrassed for asking.

"Whatever you want. He will listen and do what you ask. He knows you won't suggest anything mean or hurtful. He knows you are good. Go ahead and think to yourself what you want him to do. He will listen. He will hear you," Ruby advised.

Jojo wanted to see the swan go back into the lake and float slowly across the opposite way. She thought it would be cool to see the swan fly, too. She couldn't decide which would be better. The swan knew. While Jojo was trying to make up her mind, the swan flapped its wings, then lowered itself to the ground. Too quick to be called a flight, but more than a jump. The swan was on the ground. Walking toward the water. Once again, it left the present and entered the in-between. The night above and below. The swan moved toward the lake.

Jojo thought. Jojo watched. She wondered and hoped. The lake gladly accepted the disturbance caused by the entrance of the swan. It smoothed and supported the bird. The water magnified the presence of the beautiful one in white. Jojo focused on her desire for the swan. She wanted to keep it to herself and surprise Ruby. She didn't think she knew how, but she wanted to. She needed to show Ruby. More importantly, to show herself. Jojo spoke, "MY turn, lady. Close YOUR eyes." Ruby smiled, big time. Ruby closed her eyes. "Your hand, please," Jojo requested.

Jojo held Ruby's hand. Jojo spoke to the swan. She thought and told. Ruby saw the swan. She kept her eyes closed. Jojo closed hers, too. They watched together. Suddenly, the swan disappeared from Ruby's sight. She searched but could not see it. But Jojo saw it. Jojo smiled because she knew. Ruby did not smile. She looked but could not see.

There were no tiny ripples in the lake to show the direction the swan had taken. There was only still blackness. Its image had only been captured in time.

The moon reflected on the lake. It had moved considerably since their arrival. The moon was preparing, almost selfishly, to remove its picture from the water and slowly drag itself away, soon to be crossing different shapes, heights, and surfaces.

Some accepting its light, others blocking it, hiding what was below.

Jojo saw the moon's reflection and thought. She spoke out loud.

"NOW!" she commanded.

The center of the moon's image on the water's surface erupted. The long white neck showed first. The wings next, flapping slowly. The swan lifted its head in pride. The beautiful bird emerged from the lake entirely. Its movements removed nearly all of the lake's water from its feathers. A light film of moisture remained on the swan. The moon reflected off this moisture, ignoring the lake.

Ruby gasped at the sight, momentarily speechless. She opened her eyes, then exclaimed, "Good Lord, Jojo. That is absolutely incredible!"

The swan hovered above the water, suspended. The moon's rays came and went in various lengths and shapes from different angles and layers of the swan's feathers, creating a continually moving, multi-dimensional kaleidoscope, mystically displaying thousands of shapes and shades of silver and white. Heaven, Earth, beast, and the mind of man making it possible.

Rightly so, Jojo's face showed her pride. All glowing aside, she beamed. She didn't know how she'd done it, but she had. The swan displayed her thoughts exactly. Ruby's face was nothing more than a wide-open mouth. Like she'd stopped speaking in the middle of the word "wow."

Then, the swan disappeared. It didn't return to the lake or fly away. It just vanished. Jojo had passed her own test, but she needed a break. She had a headache. She needed to stop for now. Ruby agreed, then explained that Jojo had used areas of thinking that she had never used before. The headaches would lessen, then stop altogether in time. The mind needs exercise like the rest of the body.

Time began to move again.

Nature began to call. Ruby spoke, "Well, child. I have a bit of a dilemma. I have an old and impatient, shriveled-up bladder that is holding a Big Gulp of Dr. Pepper, no ice. I'm afraid I'm going to have to use the bushes. I'm sure you're wondering how an old lady in a wheelchair, in the bushes, in the dark, could make it happen. How 'bout you relax, sit back, and help that headache of yours while I keep one secret to myself? Sound good?" She winked at Jojo, who smiled, then took the advice, sat back, and closed her eyes.

When Ruby returned and settled back in the van, Jojo was asleep. She helped herself to one of Jojo's donuts. She thought to herself how well the girl had done. The poor kid had been through a lot. Ruby was exhausted herself, but she knew the time was short.

The increasing sound of automobiles en route to places of business indicated the day was near. The darker sky gradually transitioned from light gray to blue as the day slowly marched its way in.

The park was now open. Professionals power-walked around the lake before work. Maintenance workers drove little green trucks from one garbage can to another, swapping out full trash bags for new ones containing only static.

Ruby sadly started the van. Jojo moved, slightly turning to a more comfortable position, and then sank deeper into sleep. Ruby looked at her innocent young apprentice and thought, *Yes, sir, a gift from God she truly is.*

Ruby put the van in reverse. They were at the end of the road. It was time to turn around. It was time to go toward their destinies.

CHAPTER ELEVEN

At a street corner along the way, a young girl was selling daffodils. A large vase rested on a card table. The cardboard sign leaning against one of the table's legs stated the price—one dollar each. Ruby stopped, called the girl over, and had her pick out two of her best flowers. Ruby handed the girl a bill with Benjamin Franklin's face on the front, then said, "Keep the change, sweetie."

The young girl's smile was of greater value to Ruby than the ninety-eight dollars of change could ever have been. She took one of the flowers, rested it behind her ear, looked in the mirror, thought, *Not quite*, and then she put on a pair of sunglasses that she had purchased from a dollar store over a year back. The frames held large, dark, heart-shaped plastic lenses. She looked in the mirror again—perfect. She placed Jojo's flower in one of the Dasani bottles with about two inches of water left in the bottom. This she placed in the cupholder on Jojo's side. Then Ruby lightly tapped the sleeping girl's leg and thought, *We'd better be going.* She turned on her turn signal, looked, and re-entered traffic. Once again, they were on their way.

As soon as Ruby's van was out of sight, the young daffodil vendor wisely decided to call it a day after her first and only customer. She folded the card table and hid it and her cardboard sign in some nearby bushes, so she could open it again tomorrow. She walked in bliss, with a vase nearly full of flowers tightly gripped in one hand, the hundred-dollar bill in the other. Her mind eagerly planned ways to put her small fortune to good use.

CHAPTER TWELVE

Hablo Español

They were the first to arrive at The Garden Store, just behind Mr. Dennis. The black and white closed sign had not been turned around to the orange and white open side. The front door was unlocked. Jojo pushed it open, jingling three metal bells that hung from the inside handle, announcing their entrance. She held the door open wide for Ruby to enter easily with her wheelchair. The sound from the bells seemed to signal the store's caged birds to change their joyful songs of secrecy to ones of simplicity and repetition, meant for the ears of man.

Mr. Dennis must still be opening up or in back some-where, thought Jojo.

The pair made their way to the front of the store's birds for Jojo to practice some of what she'd learned. She could feel the air come alive. The birds immediately began to communicate with Jojo. She learned that the birds had known for a long time that one day, she would speak with them. Their talk resembled friends catching up after not seeing each other for a long time.

Satisfied, Ruby proudly watched, then said, "I'm going to use the restroom. You keep going. Take your time. Before I go, I want you to know, child, things couldn't have gone better this last night. You were, are, absolutely perfect for your calling."

Jojo noticed tears in Ruby's eyes. They looked like tiny Twin Lakes of bluish sad. Ruby was so happy she was almost crying. She made her way toward the bathroom.

Jojo continued chatting with the birds. She asked the parrot why he had never said any of the words she'd tried to teach him before. He explained to her that he had been waiting for their real conversations. The parrot wanted her to know that he was more than a tape recorder with feathers. He could think and speak in full, well-thought-out sentences, and not to brag, but he also knew how to speak Spanish. He was a bilingual bird who also had a sense of humor.

Jojo smiled. Her heartbeat was faster than normal. Happiness and excitement caused a tightness in her body that made her unable to relax, trapping a deep breath that she couldn't let go of. To compensate, she breathed more shallowly than normal.

"How's my favorite youngster today?" Mr. Dennis asked. He had walked up unnoticed due to her deep conversation.

Startled, Jojo answered, "Great, oh man, hi, Mr. Dennis. I'm here with my friend Ruby. She'll be right back. I want you to meet her. She's even older than you."

"I didn't think that was possible. Older than me, huh? I'd love to meet her. I have some things to finish up. I'll be back in a few, or I'll see you when you get ready to leave. Either way, I'll see you in a shorty," Mr. Dennis replied.

CHAPTER ? THIRTEEN

Jojo's interest returned to the birds. Soon, she was interrupted again.

"Time to go, kids," Brenda said, shocking Jojo considerably. Jojo hadn't realized that her mother, with Hudson in a shopping cart, had been standing behind her, let alone in the store, for that matter.

"What are you doing here, Mom?" Inquired an astonished Jojo.

"Don't be silly, sweetheart. Hudson and I just fin-ished picking up the things for the yard. I was letting him watch the birds before we go. Are you ready?" Brenda inquired.

"I'm here with Ruby. Can't I stay with her?" Jojo asked, becoming confused.

"Who's Ruby?" Brenda asked, somewhat perplexed.

"Mom," stated Jojo almost sarcastically.

Assuming her daughter was in the midst of make-believe, Brenda said, "Sorry. You can't stay here with this, uh, Ruby. You're going home with me and Hudson, ready?" She questioned, beginning to get a little impatient.

"I can't, Mom. Not yet," Jojo stated, becoming flustered.

"No more playing. We have things to do. It's time to go," instructed Brenda, who proceeded to take her daughter by the hand and began to lead her to the cash register.

"Please, Mom. Can't I at least say goodbye?" Jojo begged.

"That's enough. Drop it," Brenda commanded.

Hudson looked back and forth between his sister and mother, disliking the tension. His chin began to show a drip of drool from his open mouth of uncertainty.

Jojo looked in the direction of the bathroom. No sign of Ruby. Begrudgingly, she stood in line with her mother and Hudson near the cash register. When their turn came, Jojo noticed her mother had picked out the same items they had bought yesterday. The flower starts, bulbs, and seeds all appeared to be the same. When Mother paid for the items, Mr. Dennis smiled and gave Jojo and Hudson a piece of butterscotch candy. Just like yesterday.

Jojo looked backward, searching for Ruby. She couldn't see her. When they left the store, Jojo noticed that Ruby's van wasn't parked in front anymore.

After getting into her family's SUV with Mother and Hudson, the drive home was a blur to Jojo. It was a sunny summer day, but it seemed cloudy to her. Everything was mixed up.

"When we get home, can I at least go see Ruby for a minute to see why she left the store without saying goodbye? To make sure she's okay?" Jojo pleaded hopefully.

"Jojo, I don't mind playing your games with you once in a while. An imagination is a wonderful thing, but like I told you this morning, we are going to be working in the yard today. It's beautiful out. Why don't you say goodbye to Ruby now? Maybe tomorrow, if you still feel like it, you can play with her then or something. K? Sweetie?" Mother replied, looking at Jojo, trying to convince her daughter with her eyes to let it go, while inside, Brenda was beginning to worry.

"Okay," Jojo answered in her best voice of agreement while her mind tried to come up with an answer that made some kind of sense.

After driving a few blocks from The Garden Store, suddenly, sirens could be heard coming from behind the family's SUV, causing Brenda to pull to the right side of the road. Just like yesterday. Next came one, then two more police cars, which were blaring sirens and boasting red and blue lights along the way. Once again.

After it became quiet, the Cobblers continued until they were forced to stop because of a police car blocking the road. Of course, there sat the black man's car with its doors and trunk open. The man was lying on his stomach, his hands handcuffed behind him. A policeman's knee was helping to hold him down. He faced Jojo and her family. He shed a tear. After she and the man had their telepathic conversation, Jojo began looking at the car's bumper stickers until a policeman came and spoke to Mother. Next, the police car moved, and the family started driving the rest of the way home. Jojo glanced over, and sure enough, Hudson was watching Paw Patrol on the car's entertainment system while her mom continued talking.

When they pulled into their driveway, Brenda said, "Jojo, please walk Hudson into the house for me. After I unload the car, we'll have a quick lunch, then go outside."

"You got it," answered Jojo sadly. It was the same. Again.

Jojo helped Hudson walk into the house. Of course, he didn't fall, and of course, lunch was tuna sandwiches, cut diagonally, with bananas and orange juice. After the kids brought their dirty dishes to their mom, she washed them. Dried her hands on her apron, then tucked a few strands of her hair behind her ears that had fallen free.

Jojo tried to make sense of this do-over day. She thought maybe she had been or was dreaming. One thing was for sure, though; she couldn't wait to climb into the treehouse as soon as Father got home so she could see Ruby in her yard. Ruby had to have the answers. She hoped.

Next, Jojo waited with Hudson at the picnic table. Once again, Hudson jumped up and down and fell onto his bottom. Jojo carried the bouncy flat of flowers beside the flowerbeds. When she watered with the hose, a rainbow appeared. When Hudson took his turn, she told him the names of the colors in the rainbow. Hudson repeated them silently.

Ordinarily, Jojo would have been bubbly. One or two steps beyond happy. Today was different. She went through the motions she already knew would come. The day seemed to take forever. Her usual smile was replaced with tight lips and a faraway look in her eyes.

Brenda went into the house and started dinner while Jojo and Hudson watered the newly planted flowerbeds. After dinner began cooking, she stepped back into the yard and then went back inside the house. She wanted to keep an eye on Jojo without her daughter knowing she was watching her. Brenda was really worried. Ever since The Garden Store, Jojo wasn't acting like herself. There was definitely something wrong. She decided that tonight, after prayers, when the two of them were alone, she would ask what was wrong. If she didn't find out in the meantime.

A child's pain is experienced many times over by a parent who can't take it away. This was the first time Jojo had some sort of problem that she was trying to handle on her own. Brenda's eyes became misty at the unknown her daughter was struggling with, sadly accepting that she was taking her first steps at becoming an independent young lady.

Brenda made sure her eyes were clear, put a make-believe smile on her face, and entered the yard once more, unhappily accepting the fact that her children would someday cease to be children and eventually grow up.

CHAPTER FOURTEEN

After Mother complimented Jojo and Hudson on their work, the side gate opened. Trevor was home, finally.

"Dad, Dad," greeted the sister and brother at almost the same time, but for different reasons. Jojo meant well, but secretly, she knew her father's arrival meant it was time to climb into the treehouse and get a glimpse of Ruby.

She hugged her father's waist while Hudson hugged his leg. After their discussion about the bank robber, Trevor spoke, "You guys had quite a morning, then a busy afternoon in the yard. What do you say we play until supper?"

"Sure, we just finished," Jojo replied anxiously. She then thought to herself, *Yes! Finally!*

She was ready to climb into the treehouse. This was the moment Jojo had been waiting for all day. Soon, things would begin to make sense. Suddenly, she became nervous about climbing into the treehouse.

What if she climbed up and couldn't see Ruby next door? What then? Was it possible that she hadn't even met Ruby yet? What if there was no Ruby, and the long magical night had been a dream?

She finally concluded that it was best to climb the tree and find out. The worry of the unknown is often more painful than the problem itself.

Jojo climbed the tree's branches into the treehouse. She looked over at the Simons' backyard. Ruby wasn't there. She felt sick to her stomach and very tired. Too many thoughts and questions came to her mind at once. She began to cry, just like in Ruby's van last night when things became too much. Or did that even happen? She just didn't know anymore. Brenda began carrying dinner to the picnic table.

Jojo wiped her tears, then slowly climbed down from the treehouse. She wasn't hungry at all. The rest of the family ate a huge dinner of fried chicken, pork-n-beans, potato chips, green salad, and chocolate pudding. Jojo picked lightly at her dinner. When everyone had finished eating, her plate was still full.

She pushed her dinner away and said, "I feel really sick. I think I'd better go to bed."

Brenda and Trevor looked at each other. Their eyes spoke their troubled thoughts, which they chose not to voice out loud.

"I think that's the best idea I've heard all day. You look like you don't feel well. It's probably a bug of some sort. I hear there's one going around," Mother agreed. Brenda was making up the part about the bug going around to try to comfort her daughter and hoping to make herself feel a little better as well. It didn't work.

Jojo rose from the picnic table. She gave everyone a hug. Hudson kissed his sister when he received his hug, then asked, "Jojo better?" It was too cute.

"A lot better. Thanks, buddy," Jojo agreed. She smiled at her brother to worry him none, then walked toward the house.

"Put some pajamas or sweats on, sweetheart, and get into bed. I'll be up to check on you in a few," Mom called after her.

Roughly ten minutes later, Brenda went into Jojo's room and found her daughter in a deep sleep. She pulled a chair to the bed's edge and sat down. She gently placed her hand on the resting girl's forehead. She felt warm but not hot. There was no fever. With the same hand, she slowly began brushing Jojo's hair back, wishing this movement would erase whatever it was that was affecting her so. Brenda continued to sit in the chair and watched Jojo sleep. Remembering. Praying.

CHAPTER ⚰ FIFTEEN

It hadn't felt like she'd been asleep very long when Jojo was awakened by her father's voice. "Jo, wake up, kiddo."

Something wasn't right. Usually, Hudson crawling on her bed was what lured her out of sleep each morning. She always hugged him close at each day's beginning. She enjoyed his warmth and soft skin. She even appreciated the lightly sour smell that was around his neck from sweating during the night. Jojo glanced around the room. He wasn't there.

"Where's Hudson?" she asked.

"He's in his crib. We'll get him in a few," answered Trevor.

Brenda said, "Sweetheart, we have some news. Bad news, I'm afraid. You're so young. This is so hard. Jojo, please look at me."

Jojo looked into her mother's pained eyes. They were wet.

"What's wrong?" Jojo asked. "Mom?" Her spine tingled, and she suddenly became cold.

Now, Brenda's eyes broke contact. She looked down.

"Mom?" Jojo repeated. She lifted her mother's chin back up with the tips of her fingers. Looking into her eyes, she saw that she was crying.

"What's wrong?" Jojo asked again.

Now Trevor took Jojo's hand and said, "The Simons came over after dinner. Jo, Ruby died during the night." Tears began to show in his eyes.

Brenda hugged her daughter. Jojo's head rested on her mother's shoulder, her eyes staring straight ahead. She looked at the wall but wasn't paying attention to it. She began to feel her mother's tears running down her neck and onto the back of her pajamas. Jojo didn't cry. She thought. She was trying to understand.

"Ruby died during the night."

The words sounded like someone was stepping on an aluminum can inside of her head, loud and demanding attention, but they didn't hurt. And like aluminum, the words couldn't stick; they only touched her. They weren't painfully magnetic like those spoken in anger. They were the way it was. They were the truth.

It was time to look inside and see.

Suddenly, Jojo recalled the mysterious, repetitive days she'd just experienced. Maybe, just maybe, they could help make sense of things. Her parents were acknowledging Ruby's existence. She had died, so she had to have lived. They obviously wouldn't be telling her this if they hadn't met her. The recent day or two had to be understood. Was it part of a dream? If so, what part was real? When was the dream?

Most importantly, Ruby had died. They'd had such a wonderful night. Jojo had just met her. Even though their ages were so far apart, their ideas and interests were aligned. Jojo thought of the swan and

The Garden Store when things had changed and she couldn't find Ruby anymore.

"So, you remember Ruby? Right?" Jojo inquired, feeling foolish for asking but knowing she had to.

"Of course, sweetie," Brenda answered. "You just met her, and now . . ." She stopped talking.

"It's alright, Mom," Jojo interjected before realizing what she had said. Jojo felt okay for some reason, even though she had just been told the bad news. Jojo knew she needed some time alone.

Just as she readied to ask for some space to sort things out, Hudson began screaming from his crib, "Gamma, Gamma, Gamma, Ruby! Ruby!" He sounded hysterical. Both parents left Jojo's room and went to their son. He knew. He hadn't been told, but he could tell, and he did so loudly.

"Ruby-Ruby-Ruby!" he screamed, gasping between each word.

Hudson's diaper was wet. He'd had an accident, but not on purpose. Hudson was hurting. Trevor picked up his son. He held the sobbing boy to his chest, attempting to comfort him. The father's mind frantically searched for a way to pacify his child. He couldn't think of anything to help, and he was mad at himself for that. Hudson was just learning to talk. What could he tell him to make him feel better? His poor son. His poor, poor son.

Jojo came into the room. No one noticed her lightly glowing face.

"Can I hold him, Dad?" she asked. For lack of a better idea, Trevor agreed. Jojo held Hudson. He became calm in his sister's arms.

"It's okay, buddy. It's okay," Jojo's words soothed her brother.

Father and Mother both looked at one another in amazement and mutual pride. They put their arms around each other in support and much-needed temporary relief.

"I'm going to take him to my room for a bit," Jojo said, "to show him everything's going to be just fine."

"Sure, kiddo," Trevor replied, now even more surprised at his daughter's strength.

Hudson held close to his sister, who made him feel much better. They went into Jojo's room. She closed the door, laid him down, and changed his diaper. When he was dry, Hudson reached his arms toward his sister. She picked him up and continued to hold him close. Brenda and Trevor whispered to each other, still in their bedroom, standing near Hudson's crib.

"It obviously hasn't sunk into Jojo yet," Trevor said.

"I know. She seems to be the strongest one in the family right now. I'm worried about the fall when it does register. We're going to have to keep an eye on her," Brenda finished.

"Here, here," agreed Trevor.

In her room, Jojo was now rocking her little brother further and further away from sadness. Back to the slumber he was in before rising to the news that had upset him so. Quietly, Jojo told Hudson that she would be there to welcome him at his next awakening. The fresh grin on his face showed he understood, even though he was sound asleep. She laid him down to rest.

CHAPTER SIXTEEN

With Hudson asleep, Jojo changed out of her pajamas. When she put on the cut-off jeans she had been
wearing the previous day, she felt something in the
front pocket. Jojo reached in and pulled out a pack of
string cheese. It was the one she hadn't eaten. The
one from the convenience store. So, it had happened!

She opened the package, then put her nose very
close to the white cheese and smelled it. She always
did that when no one was looking. She tore off a
couple of strands and put them in her mouth, slowly

chewed, and thought. She gazed out the window and thought some more.

It had happened. The proof she needed had just been shown to her. She was eating it. The night with Ruby had happened. The convenience store, Wapato Lake Park, the swan . . . But somehow, from the time she went into the store, Ruby seemed to have disappeared. Then it was like that day ended, and the one before started all over again. How could that be? Why?

It's because I ran out of time, child. Ruby's voice came to Jojo inside her thoughts.

"Ruby! Oh, Ruby! I'm so glad. I'm totally messed up, but it's so good to hear you," Jojo said out loud.

Listen, child, remarked Ruby again through thought.

"No! You listen, Ruby," Jojo cut her off, "I want you to think about what I—what my family and I have gone through. I don't even know where to start. It's like you expect so much out of me. I'm only eleven. My family doesn't even know you, but everybody's crying. I have been through more happy and sad, up and down, feeling like I don't even know since I've met you. I'm reliving days. I'm talking to owls and a Spanish-speaking parrot, of all things. Hudson barely saw you once, and he's, like, traumatized or something. He's almost potty trained, but he wet himself. Mom and Dad are both crying. I'm not, but I was."

Jojo stopped speaking. She caught herself. She had meant what she said, but she had pushed too far, and she knew it. Ruby knew, too, but Ruby wasn't mad. She understood.

Jojo spoke again., "I am so sorry. You died. I mean, you're dead! Oh Ruby, how? Why did you have to die now? Did it hurt? I-I mean, we just met. I need you. I am so sorry about the way I just spoke to you. I must sound like a total jerk. I do, huh? Like I only care about myself. I am SO SORRY."

Ruby's voice rang in her head. *I understand. It's okay. You have nothing to be sorry about. I am sorry, Jojo. For what you are going through. No, it did not hurt. It was like taking off heavy, dirty, old clothes and putting clean ones on. And yes, you are right. This was a lot for anyone to deal with, let alone an eleven-year-old. I only wish I would have known, but that's the catch. It makes it all worthwhile. No one does. We aren't supposed to. If people did know ahead of time, most would* live inappropriately and try to make things right just before the end. There would be no purpose for Faith. There would be no reward. It would just end at the end.

What I'm taking the long way to say, I guess, is Jojo, I truly am sorry. Sorry for any stress and problems I have caused you or your family. You are all hurting, yes, because of me and also because you love one another. Your parents are hurt because they feel you are. You hurt because Hudson does. And you know what? Hudson is hurt because he's sad for you. He really doesn't know it, but it's so.

Jojo, last night was my last night. In a way. There is no other person I would rather have spent it with than you. The way we did. Partway through our time at the park, my time came. I'm not allowed to say when, but it did. It was then that there had to be a shift, a pause. Your learning wasn't complete yet. To allow us to finish, time stopped just for us. It kept going for everyone else, though. We, no, you didn't notice it then, and it was worth it. When you pierced the center of the moon's reflection with the swan, that was the most beautiful thing I have ever seen.

You used your power on your own. Kind of like when you first learn to ride a bike. You know the basics:

balance, pedaling, stopping. Then it's up to you to practice. No one can do that part for you. It's just you and the bike. Anyway, while you learned, time continued everywhere except with us. Then, when I left, after my borrowed time, you could say—ha, ha—yeah, I know; that was awful, Ruby chuckled at her own joke, then continued telepathically, *The only way to make things whole was for you to re-enter during another pause while you were asleep. You went back a day, then you caught up and re-entered completely while you slept.*

"Yeah. It's, like, I get it, but I don't. I don't think I'm supposed to yet," Jojo answered. "Ruby, if I tried to explain what happened last night, no one would believe me. People would think I'm crazy. I know that if I hadn't experienced it, I wouldn't believe it myself. Somehow, I know I'm not supposed to think about it for now. I learned so much about myself, and I feel different now. More relaxed. It's like I know everything will be okay, no matter what."

That's called inner peace, child. Deep down, that's what everyone is after. You will never lose it, either. Sometimes, it will increase, and other times, it may dwindle only to return many times over.

I want you to remember I am always with you. When you think of or speak to me, I will always hear you and respond. We went over so much last night. You will have more and more questions. As you learn something new, many more questions will come. I will answer them all gladly. It's my new job, Your Guardian Angel and Advisor. Sounds like an important title. A responsibility and pleasure I have looked forward to my entire Earthly life, Ruby thought to Jojo.

Hudson began to stir. He looked at Jojo and, clear as day, said, "Jojo better?"

Gosh, that kid is so cute, thought Ruby.

"He sure is," Jojo replied as she picked him up.

Well, child, I can see that you have your hands full. Time for me to go. No, that's not the right word. It's time for me to step back until you need me, Ruby concluded.

Jojo smiled and said, "Yes, Hudson. Jojo's all better. I sure love you, buddy. Do you want some string cheese?"

* * *

It is absolutely necessary to shed tears in life. This cleanses the eyes, opening them to new perspectives and helping them to clearly see the good in life. Proving true, it is impossible to experience true happiness unless moments of sadness are met occasionally along the way.

CHAPTER SEVENTEEN

The SUV slowly pulled to the side of the narrow road, allowing just enough room for others to be able to pass.

Brenda turned off the engine, then spoke, "You sure you still want to go alone?"

"Yeah, I feel like I'm supposed to. If I change my mind, I'll come back and get you, though," Jojo replied.

"Okay, I'll leave my window down. Just give me a holler if so. Okay?" Brenda finished.

Jojo nodded and removed the yellow flower from the Dasani bottle that had been serving as a vase. She opened her door and then began to walk. She stopped at the edge of the fresh soil and set the flower down in front of the carved stone marker. A cloud drifted in front of the sun, casting a shadow on the ground. This gave the impression the temperature had dropped. Jojo could feel goosebumps on her arms. She looked up at the cause. The wind resumed. The cloud moved and was forgotten almost as quickly as it was noticed. Just like goosebumps. She began to nudge the loose dirt with the tips of her tennis shoes. She looked at the headstone, which read, "Here lies Ruby Danford, born June 5, 1941. Beloved mother and friend."

Don't believe everything you read, child. Ruby's voice could be heard in Jojo's thoughts.

"Ruby! Well, how do you like Heaven so far?" Jojo asked.

Definitely worth the wait. Almost sorry I had to. It takes some adjusting, of course. Some things you never forget, though, answered Ruby. She then continued, *By the way, how did you know I like daffodils?*

"I didn't. To be honest, I'm regifting," replied Jojo, "You don't mind, do you?"

Mind? Of course not. As they say, it's the thought. And thank you, by the way. Do you think the person who gave it to you would be hurt if they found out? Ruby asked.

"I don't know, are you?" Jojo joked.

Since I got it back so quickly. I'm going to pretend like I lent it to you, laughed Ruby. *Seriously, child, how are you? Your family?*

"Hudson seems to be doing good. Especially when I'm with him. Mom and Dad are totally freaked out, worrying about me, of course. And me, I'm adjusting, I guess you could say, considering a week ago I had never even met you, and then I did, and now it's like I've known you my whole life. We shared the most awesome night when I found out I have some magical powers, then you died, and now I'm at your grave, and I'm talking to you like you're still alive. Considering I'm only eleven years old, I'm pretty dang good, I'd say. No, Ruby . . . I mean, I'm serious, but I'm teasing too. Somehow, I know everything will be okay. I'm going over to your house—I mean Lorraine's—when we leave here. I guess you wanted me to, huh?" Finished Jojo.

Yes, I'd be pleased if you did. My daughter has some things to tell you. Maybe you should get going. I can see your mom's still worried about you, Ruby observed.

Jojo glanced over at the SUV. Her mother, who had been looking in her direction, turned and looked away, acting like she hadn't been. "You're right. I'd better go. Nice place, by the way," Jojo joked about the cemetery.

Watch it, child. Besides wilting flowers, tears, and memories, cemeteries also contain lots of patience and time. There's plenty of room for everyone here, Ruby joked back.

* * *

As soon as Jojo entered the Simons' home, Lorraine hugged her and said, "Jojo, I'm so glad you're here. You went out and visited Ruby, I take it?"

"Yeah, Mom took me. Ruby had bought me a flower that night, and I still had it. It was like she knew, so I kind of gave it back," Jojo replied.

"That was thoughtful, and I agree. I believe she did know. That's what I'd like to talk to you about. Make yourself comfortable, and please, have a seat." Lorraine motioned to her sofa.

"Would you like something to drink? We have Dr. Pepper, bottled water, and I'm pretty sure there's some grape juice left," she offered.

"Grape juice sounds good," Jojo said gratefully.

"You got it. I'll be right back," answered Lorraine. When she returned from the kitchen, she put the two glasses of juice down on the coffee table. She sat in a chair facing Jojo.

Lorraine recounted the story of how Ruby had flown her airplane to an extremely high, unsafe altitude and the engines stalled. She did everything she could to restart them, but when that failed, she fought to keep the plane level and glide it as far as possible before she was forced to eject. Getting to her parachute and taking the leap took too much time and didn't leave the chute ample time to fully deploy. It did slow her rapid descent, however, and saved her life, but the bone-crushing impact left her paralyzed from the waist down. She had been confined to a wheelchair ever since. Ruby felt entirely responsible for the accident. Even when the insurance company investigating the accident found fault with the airplane, Ruby blamed herself. Finally, Ruby's lawyer convinced her to let him handle the matter and help cover her future medical bills. He was also able to get Ruby a large settlement awarded from the plane manufacturer. Ruby was wise with her settlement. Instead of keeping the money to herself like most people would, she used part of the money to create a college scholarship. Another portion she donated to a flight school to enable people to learn to become pilots who wouldn't have been able to otherwise. She put the rest into sound investments and was able to live off the interest comfortably. When she passed away, she was a very rich woman. Anyway, Jojo, do you remember the other night when you first met Ruby and the two of you became acquainted in our backyard?' Lorraine asked.

"Of course," replied the young girl.

Lorraine continued, "You made quite an impression on her that night. I have never seen her happier than she was after meeting you. You see, Jojo, as soon as she met you, she knew you were the *one.* The one she had patiently searched her entire adult life for. Mom always joked that her wheelchair gave her a front-row seat, a better view, if you will, into other people's hearts than most. She was an expert at reading people. She took on the responsibility, and she made it her life's mission to find the person best suited to receive her inheritance and manage it properly. Someone filled with kindness, similar interests, and beliefs. After your mom called you home that night, Ruby and I spoke for more than an hour. Well . . . It was more like she talked, and I listened, actually." Lorraine laughed, and so did Jojo.

Lorraine went on, "Jojo, Mom said you beam a warm, golden energy that walks before you. She said you are already rich by the treasures that live inside of you and that there is no selfishness in you. There is only love for others. She said that because you already know how to manage true riches at just eleven years old, when you turn eighteen, and then twenty-one and beyond, she felt that you were the best one to manage all of her money. She thought you would direct it and spend it similar to how she would, yet in your own way. Do you understand what I am saying, Jojo? You are a very, very rich young lady. You're a millionaire many times over. At certain age markers through-out your life, like eighteen and twenty-one, differ-ent amounts of money will be released to you to use as you see fit. You can study at any college you want, but Ruby also wanted to make it clear that it's just as important, maybe even more so, for you to continue being the happy kid you are now and enjoy each day as it comes. It's okay to think about the future, to close your eyes and dream, but it's also very important to never lose sight of the now—of the moment at hand."

Jojo and Lorraine looked into one another's eyes, and they both smiled. Jojo slowly began processing the news she had just been told. A flood of happy thoughts filled her mind about college and being rich, then she caught herself and remembered the advice she had just been told. "Never lose sight of the moment at hand." To do so, she momentarily closed her eyes, casting her thoughts aside. She opened them once more and continued looking at Lorraine. Neither one spoke, allowing a silence to enter the room that was much more welcome than awkward. Sometimes, just listening to the silence can be much more pow-erful and meaningful than even the most beautifully spoken words.

EPILOGUE

Forty Years Later

The charter plane had left Anchorage nearly an hour before. Aboard the aircraft, six disabled teens were eagerly looking forward to the upcoming two weeks they were going to spend in an isolated area known as Twin Lakes. This adventure followed their ship ride from Seattle, a first for all of the teens on the small plane.

"I know how much you all enjoyed the cruise. Everyone did so well on the boat. Nobody even got seasick. I am so proud of you. The area we are going to is the most beautiful, peaceful place. You will just love it. There are cabins and canoes, plus a couple of docks to fish from on one of the two lakes loaded with trout. We'll have scavenger hunts and campfires with marshmallows every night." Jojo's face shone. Her eyes lit up when she spoke to this year's guests.

The annual trip to Alaska was one of many programs that Jojo had created to give disabled young people similar experiences to those without disabilities as a tribute honoring Ruby's life.

Using gifts and insights she'd learned from Ruby, Jojo had dedicated her life to helping people whose paths were sometimes blocked or made difficult by challenges. She did not dwell on the disabilities of the youth aboard the plane. She knew how to look deeper. She saw the inside. The real person. Jojo knew that with creativity and effort, people with disabilities could live normal, full lives, no matter what someone's definition of normal was.

"If everyone could please make sure to have your seatbelts fastened. It may get bumpy for a bit." The pilot's voice came through a speaker to his seven passengers. Even though the speaker was crackly, Jojo could tell the pilot's voice was strained.

The trip had been smooth up until now. The sky was light blue. A periodic cloud was just a reminder they still existed on the unblemished horizon. Jojo thought the pilot's message did not make sense, so she went to investigate.

"You guys hang tight. I'm going to find out how long we can expect turbulence and how much further to Twin Lakes. I think we're close," Jojo said to the group. She made sure all six were wearing their seatbelts and smiled at them reassuringly. She entered the cockpit and shut the door behind her.

"So, Denny, spill it. What's wrong?" Jojo inquired sympathetically. Jojo and the pilot, Denny Lund, had known each other since flight school. When Jojo had approached him years earlier with her plans for the youth summer getaway, Denny had offered his services and the use of his plane free of charge. They had been close friends for nearly three decades.

"Honestly, I don't think it's anything," Denny replied. "I'm feeling a little off, is all. I'm just coming back after the flu. As the saying goes, 'better safe than sorry.'"

"I think I'll stay up here and keep you company," Jojo suggested.

"You'll do no such thing. You enjoy those kids as much as they enjoy you. Maybe more. Now get back there, Jo. I'm fine, I swear. Just cautious is all," Denny insisted, faking a smile to comfort Jojo.

Jojo knew her friend wasn't feeling well and he was pretending to feel better than he was, but not wanting to worry the teens, she re-entered the cabin smiling.

"So, I have to tell you. I don't mind putting worms on your hooks for fishing. I'll even take to rowing a canoe once in a while, but all campfire stories are up to you guys. Agreed?" Jojo teased, trying to lighten the mood.

"Agreed!"

"Sure thing, Miss Cobbler!"

"Sure!" came the teen's replies.

Jojo began informing the teens about the Twin Lakes area. She explained the unusually friendly wild-life there and shared that on clear nights, the stars were so dense and hung so low, you could easily read from their light. Jojo encouraged it. She even brought certain books she wanted them to explore at night together. She stated that words read under starlight became magical and could never be forgotten.

Once again, the pilot's voice came through the speaker. "Jo?" he spoke, then abruptly stopped. The front of the plane started going down. Something was wrong.

"Hang tight, everyone. I have to go up front again," Jojo said to the teens, who were now wearing pale faces of panic.

In the cockpit, Denny was slumped over in his seat, unconscious.

He had a heart attack, child. Why don't you take over the controls? Ruby said to Jojo as clearly as if she was right beside her. *Radio ahead to Twin Lakes. There's another plane there preparing to leave. Tell them to wait and let them know about the emergency. They are going to have one unexpected extra passenger. He'll be going to the hospital in Sitka,* Ruby finished.

Jojo sat down next to Denny. She took command of the plane, bringing it level again to the cheers of the teens in the cabin. Next, she put her hand on Denny's sweaty forehead. He slowly came to, laid his head back on the seat, then closed his eyes.

Jojo whispered, "You hang on there, Denny. You're going to be just fine." Denny seemed to smile at her voice, although extremely weakly.

"You're going to be just fine," Jojo repeated.

I don't know what I'd do without you, Ruby, Jojo thought.

Without me, are you kidding? I'm just a yackity old lady. Heck, I'm not even alive, well, technically anyway, Ruby answered Jojo's thought. Jojo smiled. *Do you realize you just saved eight lives, including your own?* Ruby asked.

"I don't see it that way. I'm just glad Denny will get cared for properly and that these kids will be able to experience camp like they deserve. I'm happy that things will work out for all of them," Jojo responded.

You are way too modest, Ruby said. *Jojo, you are a hero. You are my hero.*

"Come on, I just leveled off the plane," Jojo muttered.

That's what I mean. It has always been your intentions. You put others before yourself. You always have, and you always will. Today is a prime example. Yes, today you were heroic. The Good Lord knows you were. All those aboard the plane, including myself, know what you did. Jojo, it is your everyday life. You bring about positive changes in other people's lives, seeing the good in people and helping them to see it themselves. This

*is what makes you a hero. That has always been your
destiny.*

* * *

The gates between Earth and Heaven are always open
to those who seek. Just inside, some Angels greet and
welcome while others, like Ruby, offer prayers and
wisdom to those whose time has not yet come.

AUTHOR'S NOTE

Many of the characters mentioned in this book were inspired by real people who positively impacted my life. Most notably, this book was written for my daughter, Destiny. In addition, Jojo's brother is named after my grandson, Hudson, and Ruby's character was named after one of my closest friend's mothers. Brenda's teacher, Mrs. Damon, was named after my third-grade teacher, who happened to be my teacher during the 1976-77 school year when our country was celebrating its bicentennial birthday. Ms. McCormick was not only the name of Ruby's teacher in Chapter 1, but she was also my fourth-grade teacher. Together, Mrs. Damon and Ms. McCormick made a lasting impression on me and brightened my academic career. I'd also like to highlight Mrs. Nugent, the teacher in Jojo's homeschool assignment, who was named after my high school writing teacher.

The pilot, Denny Lund, honors a friend of my father who lived in our neighborhood. He was a pilot in real life, but unfortunately, he passed away in a plane crash when I was a young child.

Lastly, when I was a baby, I was adopted from an orphanage by the kindest woman you'd ever hope to meet, named Ruth, and her husband, Bruce. Bruce's parents became Grandpa and Grandma McGinnis. Their home was my favorite place to visit as a child, and hands down, they were the best people I have ever met. Even though they've been in Heaven for a very long time now, I still think of and speak to them almost every day.

In the Book of Ruth in the Bible, Ruth's mother and father-in-law's names were Naomi and Elimelech. Giving Brenda's grandparents those same names in Chapter 5 is my way of honoring my parents and also my grandparents.

Every one of us experiences unique and interesting lives. I encourage all of you, dear readers, to keep your memories and loved ones alive in your own special way with your gift of writing.

Thanks so much everyone. You've all been great!

—Corwin

ABOUT AUTHOR

Author **Corwin McGinnis** is a lifelong Washington State resident who makes his home in beautiful Ocean Shores with his soulmate Kristin and Buck, the dog. Combined, the couple have ten children who also call Western Washington home. Besides writing, Corwin is also a real estate investor, but it's his involvement with NAMI—The National Alliance on Mental Illness—that he is most proud of. Corwin makes it his personal mission to help with suicide prevention and awareness on the local level.

"Please always remember, you are not alone, and you are truly loved beyond measure."